A BLADE TO SILENCE THE SCREAMS

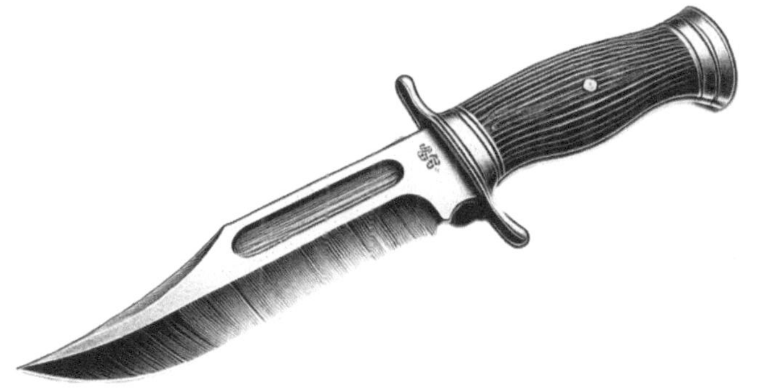

A BLADE TO SILENCE THE SCREAMS

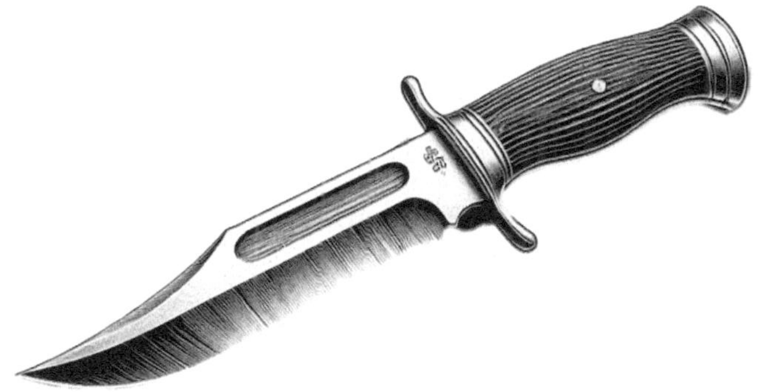

Tom Deady

CEMETERY DANCE PUBLICATIONS

Baltimore

2024

Cemetery Dance Publications
132B Industry Lane, Unit #7
Forest Hill, MD 21050
www.cemeterydance.com

Trade Paperback Edition

ISBN:
978-1-964780-09-2

Contents

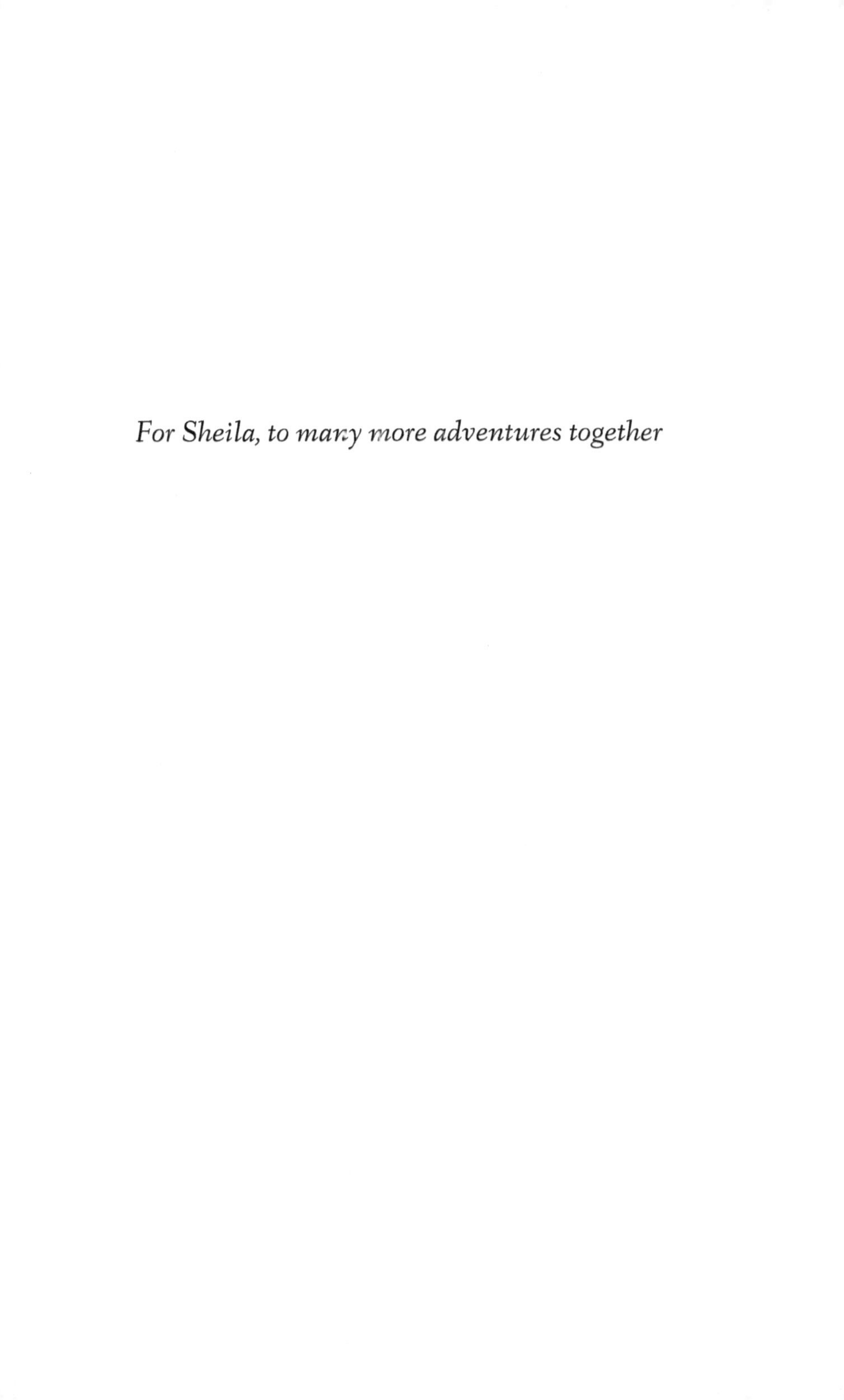

For Sheila, to many more adventures together

A BLADE TO SILENCE THE SCREAMS

Tom Deady

The shadow likes the feel of the knife in his hand. It is power, an extension of his body. The need to wield that power, unleash that *potential*, is overwhelming. It's the only way to quiet the terrible screams that deafen him and send waves of unbearable pain through his head. He's not bloodthirsty, not even excessively violent. He just does what he needs to get through the night. For some it's women, for many it's whiskey, and for others it's gambling. For the shadow, it's the blade. The weight of it is comforting.

The possibilities it holds are exciting. It is both his salvation and his doom.

He clamps a hand on the sleeping man's mouth and makes a deft movement with his other, the one holding the blade, to spectacular results. As a hot arc of blood shoots into the air, the man's eyes open wide, searching. They find the shadow and open wider, questioning. *Does he recognize me despite the bandit's mask?* Freshets of his lifeforce spray the shadow, the walls, the bed. Strong at first, he grunts and reaches for the hand clamped on his mouth. As he starts to weaken, he slaps at the shadow, then an idea seems to occur to him. He tries to stem the flow of blood by placing his hands over the gaping second mouth the blade has fashioned. It's no use: blood squirts through his fingers. All he's accomplished is to change the pattern it makes on the walls and the sheets. His body trembles, then convulses. The spray peters out to a bubbling flow as his hands fall away and the light escapes his eyes.

The woman next to him hasn't moved throughout the procedure. *Perhaps too much chloroform has stopped her heart.* It's been known to happen but the idea is disappointing. The shadow drifts over to her side of the bed now that the main threat has been dispatched. The chloroform-soaked rag is still draped across the lower half of her face. He reaches down and pulls it away, as gentle as a lover. She wrinkles her nose and turns her head from side to side as if perhaps he's tickled her, then she is still.

The shadow leans in close to take in her features. She is beautiful in the classic sense. This is purely an intellectual determination made from years of watching others, studying their behavior, listening to their conversations: beauty holds no sway over the shadow. It is as unimportant as the color of a person's hair or eyes, or how short or tall they stand. All that matters is the light in their eyes, and his power—his and the blade's—to extinguish it. And when he finds the right one, the screams will be gone for good.

She breathes evenly and her eyes shift rapidly beneath her thin lids.

"What are you dreaming about, my lady?"

Lines crease her forehead as if she's heard. *And why wouldn't the voice of a strange figure in her bedroom in the middle of the night startle her?*

Pale moonlight filters through the flimsy curtains, painting her face with a queer bluish tint as the shadow waits for her eyes to open. He needs to see them. Maybe she's the one.

The dry desert wind whips pellets of sand against the farmhouse, the sound both soothing and agitating. He ponders the paradox but can't make sense of it. He's tired. So very tired. Thunder rumbles in the distance; monsoon season is upon Sundown, the much-needed rain coming almost every night for the past week.

A smell rises in the stuffy room. Unsurprising, considering the man shat himself as he died. A lot of them do. Thunder rumbles again, closer now. The woman's eyes flutter, then open. The shadow doesn't know if this is due to the approaching storm or the stench of her dead husband, but she's awake. And she's afraid.

"It's all right," he says, "everything is all right."

She opens her mouth and lets loose a scream so shrill the windows threaten to shatter. She flails around a bit, but she is a small-framed woman and easy enough to wrangle. Eventually she realizes her futility and stops. Her eyes are wild, and he feels himself stir. But that's not what he's come for.

"What do you want?" Somehow, her voice is calm, despite her peril.

"It's not what I want," he says, matching her docile tone, "it's what I need."

She seems to consider that, then says, "And what is it you need?"

"Peace," he says, as if that will explain it all to her. Again, she considers his words before answering.

"What brings you peace?"

"Silence," he says immediately.

Despite the situation, she almost smiles. "No place for silence like the desert."

The shadow shakes his head. She doesn't get it. "It's not silence out there I need, it's silence in here." He brings the bloody knife to his lips and mimes a *ssh*. Her eyes widen but she doesn't react beyond that.

"What brings you the silence you need?"

This time it is the shadow who smiles. She's biding her time, trying to survive. *She thinks she can change my mind.* She is better at it than most. She isn't crying or sniffling and doesn't have snot running down her face. And she hasn't offered her body, another silly ploy the chosen have been known to try on occasion. "I don't know," he says, and it is God's honest truth.

Her face changes, hardens. "Then why are you here?"

The shadow flinches a bit. This is new. Different. Her voice is full of bitterness and vitriol. This one has more spirit than all the others. Is it a sign? "I have to keep searching," he says.

Her eyes dart over to where her husband lies. No doubt she already knows of his demise; the stink of blood and shit and piss is unmistakable. Every farmer's wife recognizes it. But it's as though she needs to see, however unprepared she might be. Right on cue, there comes a sort of gagging noise that turns into sobs. Still, she doesn't fall completely apart. When she turns her face back to the shadow it is so full of hatred it gives him a chill. "Lower your mask so I can see the face of my cowardly murderer." When he doesn't reply, her eyes narrow. "I don't believe you're searching for anything, mister. I believe you tell yourself that, so that when you look in the mirror, you don't have to see the deranged savage you are. *Can* you look in the mirror, or are you too disgusted with yourself?"

He thrusts the knife into her throat; the only enjoyment he gets out of it is the hot bath of blood that drenches his face. Before he has a chance to wipe the gore from his eyes, the light has gone out of hers. His rage overtakes him, and he uses the knife as he has never done before, slashing and hacking until his arm shakes from exhaustion and his sweat mixes with the blood that is covering him. He screams in agony at the voices in his head, louder than ever now. Instead of quieting them, he's only managed to quiet this one hateful bitch who taunted him and mocked him until...until this. With a final primal cry, he plunges the knife into her chest and pulls, tears, shreds, ripping her open down to her navel. Flaps of flesh lay open, exposing ropy pink things and steaming guts. It takes all his remaining strength, and the sight of her insides is no more satisfying than her death. Wearily, he stands. The rest is going to be tedious work but at least it's something to focus on.

He fetches the two jugs of kerosene he'd left in the front yard and begins to pour it liberally, starting in the bedroom—the kill room—and working his way down to the kitchen. He tosses the empty jugs on the floor and steps outside. He lights an old lantern he'd found in the house, careful not to set himself on fire, and tosses it through the open doorway, stepping back further as he does. There is an enormous WHOOMP and a blast of heat as the house ignites. The fuel burns first, emitting a bitter odor, but once the wood catches, the aroma is rather pleasant. It reminds him of his younger days - campfires and kerosene lanterns.

He backs away as the heat grows uncomfortable. At the edge of the yard, just before he enters the woods that will conceal his departure, he turns to take one last look at the flames. His heart leaps, threatening to smash into his ribcage. His hand instinctively goes to his chest as if to hold himself together. Silhouetted against the flames in one of the upstairs windows is a figure. *It can't be,* he thinks. *I know the Wrights live there alone. Well, lived.* He closes his eyes, willing this to be his imagination or some demented manifestation of his guilt, but when he opens them, the figure is still there. Small. *Tiny,* in fact. Tiny, and now burning. When the flames shift, growing brighter, just before they take the figure, it causes another awful disturbance in the shadow's chest.

He takes a step toward the burning edifice, now a funeral pyre for both the dead and the soon to be dead—just as the roof collapses. A shower of orange sparks joins purple veins of lightning to illuminate the night. The eerie light turns the blood-soaked shadow a color he's never seen before. *The color of death,* he thinks, sniffing the air for a taste of burning flesh.

I'M SITTING AT MY DESK, CHAIR TIPPED BACK ON two legs and feet perched among the messy clutter on the desktop. The coffee cups—some empty, others coated with brown grime and growing a fuzz of green—the greasy, fly-covered wrappers from long-since-eaten lunches, and of course, endless paperwork I should be working on. My head is tilted back, hat low on my fore-head, to get away with fake-sleeping. Why sleep when I can stay wide awake and watching? And I'm always watching.

The door flies open and Billy Snow bursts into the room amidst a cloud of dust and hysteria. I push my hat back and look up. How can there be so much dust after the heavy rain the night before? But in Sundown, Arizona, dust comes cheap and easy despite the wet weather.

I'm used to Billy's half-deranged excitement, the way his eyes dart everywhere at the same time. Billy's always been an excitable fucker, speaking with that wide-eyed intensity usually reserved for children and drunks. Something different, something unsettling. I whip my feet off the desk and lean forward. There is fear in Billy's eyes, and despite the kid's high-strung personality, he is never afraid. Before I can ask what is wrong, he speaks.

"Trouble out at the Wrights' place. Fire."

Fire isn't uncommon—the dry desert heat doesn't mix well with campfires and careless smokers—but this makes the third in as many months. "The Wrights?"

Billy shakes his head. "Both dead," he says quietly. He shuffles his feet, looking anywhere but at me.

There's something in the kid's eyes. Something I don't like because I've never seen it on him. "What is it, Billy?" The young man licks his lips but says nothing. "Spit it out, son," I say, "won't do either of us any good for you to keep it in."

"The Wrights," Billy says, his face etched with pain,

"they had kin stayin' with them. A niece, I think. Pretty little girl..."

My heart clenches. Death is hard no matter what, but kids dying is just wrong. Billy's eyes go watery and I try my darndest to stop my own vision from blurring. "Damn it, Billy. That's awful—"

Billy's head snaps up, eyes clearing. "No, thing is, she ain't dead, John. But...but she's burnt up pretty good. Doc's with her now."

The puzzle pieces start coming together. Billy does odd jobs all over town: repairs, harvesting, whatever people need. He must have been doing something for Doc when the girl was brought in. Whenever he's stuck for work, he hangs out at the sheriff's; Billy wants to be a lawman. Sheriff Toliver puts him out most days but I don't mind the company. "Will she..."

"Doc says it's fifty-fifty." Billy shakes his head briskly, anger setting into his boyish face. "But she ain't gonna be that pretty little girl anymore."

Something hot and greasy forms in my gut. I stare hard at Billy and feel that slippery thing slither around. "Billy?" There is more. There has to be—the kid is holding back. Christ, what else can there be?

"Melanie—the little girl—she said the Wrights were killed before the fire started."

"Killed?" I say, getting to my feet. "What do you mean?" Billy's jaw clenches, like a cow chewing her cud.

"The girl was all out of control when they brought her to Doc's—"

"Who brought her?" *Jesus, Billy, get to the fucking point.*

"The Wrights' neighbors—Amos Jones and his boy—they saw the fire. They went over there when they seen the roof collapse. Lucky, though, the storm came and worked on putting out the fire." He is wringing his hands, as if he's trying to wipe off something sticky. "Anyway, she was mostly screaming and crying, you know, cuz of the pain. The doc, he gave her something, maybe laudanum, and she started settling down. But right before she finally dozed off she said, 'The Devil kilt my auntie and uncle. Kilt them with his claws then set hellfire to the farmhouse.'"

I relax. It sounds more like the laudanum talking than the little girl. "Okay, Billy," I say, not wanting to upset the boy any further by disputing the story, "I'll head on over to Doc's."

"How is she, Doc?" The medic holds up one finger, a motion I take to mean I better let him finish what he is doing. He is leaning over Melanie, wrapping a bandage around her face and head. When he is done, he uses a scalpel to fashion eyeholes in the bandages so the girl can see when she comes to.

"She's in rough shape, John, but stable," he says.

Funny thing about Doc, he calls everyone by their name, not their title. I'm John, not Deputy. Spirit, the barkeep at the saloon, is always Walter. I'm not sure if they call him Spirit because that's what he serves or because he is practically an albino, ghost-pale. Anyway, I always find it ironic since everyone calls him Doc. As a matter of fact, I ain't sure what Doc's name really is.

When Doc steps away from the bed, I get my first clear view of the girl. The fire has ravaged her. It isn't just her face that is ruined, her torso and arms are heavily bandaged. The skin poking out from under them looks like a melted candle. Her hands have somehow been spared from the flames.

"Fucking Jesus," I mutter, turning away, thankful that the sheet covers the rest of her. "Is she going to make it?" I don't want to look at her but can't help myself.

"Too early to tell," Doc says, straightening out some of his equipment on the table next to the bed.

Doc is a man of few words, straight to the point. He might sound gruff to those who don't know him, but the old man has a heart of gold. He's taken care of everyone in Sundown for as long as I can remember. *What the fuck are we gonna do when Doc is too old to practice?*

Sundown isn't exactly rich with medical types.

"The burns are only part of it," Doc continues, "she's been traumatized by what happened. Even if the physical ailments heal up..." He shakes his head. "I just don't know."

The helplessness in his usually stoic tone fills me with sadness. Not just for the little girl, but for Doc having to deal with the damage caused by so many ruthless people. I get to do something about it: justice, vengeance, whatever. The doc, though, he just has to clean up after them.

"Billy said she was conscious. Talking?"

Doc gives me a look that isn't hard to read. "Don't believe the ramblings of a victim of such violence." Billy is known to be excitable, yes, but also known for stretching the truth.

I nod. "Any other injuries? Besides the burns?"

Doc's countenance hardens. "Isn't that enough?"

I have no answer. It hurts my heart to see her like this, her limp form on the bed. "How long do you suspect she'll be out for?"

"Several hours. She was suffering. I gave her an adult dose so settle her." While he speaks, he never stops appraising his patient. "A while," he says.

"Thanks, Doc," I say, "for taking care of her, and for the information. I'm going to head out to what's left of the house, maybe talk to Amos and his boy."

Doc keeps vigil, as if taking his eyes off her might be all it takes for her to slip away. He raises his hand without turning. I leave, more shaken than when I'd gone in.

THE REMAINS OF THE WRIGHTS' FARMHOUSE STAND stark against the pale afternoon sky like a blackened skeleton. The roof has partially collapsed, but most of it is still standing. I approach cautiously, unsure just how stable the structure is. The rain has saved what it could, but I ain't interested in being another of the fire's victims. "You smell that?"

Billy is staring at the house with that sort of dumbfounded look that's become his trademark. It fools a lot of folks, but I ain't one of them. Billy takes some exaggerated sniffs, then shrugs. "Burnt wood," he says, as if I'm some sort of feeble-minded idiot.

"Try again," I say patiently.

Billy inches closer, then crouches down by the front porch. "Kerosene," he says, "and too damn much of it to be from a lantern." The boy might make a decent deputy one day. "It weren't no devil that burnt the house down."

I smile but there is no humor behind it. "Not the kind of devil Reverend Killion preaches about," I say, "but a fucking devil just the same."

Billy's face lights up, "You think it was Indians?"

Fuckin' hell. "No reason to think so. And kerosene isn't their way of making fires. No, not the Indians." I stare Billy down. "And don't you go talkin' like that when we get to town. Last thing we need."

Billy frowns. "What next?"

"Let's go have a chat with Amos and his boy and see what we can see."

Billy is quiet as they ride toward Amos's farm. "What's on your mind, kid?"

"Just tryin' to make sense of it all. The fire, the Wrights, Melanie...fuck's sake, John."

Had anyone smelled kerosene at the other fires? Probably not, even if it was there. Tragic accidents are commonplace, no reason anyone would think the fires were anything but another notch on that gun belt.

Billy finally speaks, and I realize I've being doing what most everyone in town does: underestimating him. "John, do you think the same person set those other fires? You know, to cover up killings?"

"I'd say it's even odds, Billy." We ride the rest of the way in silence.

Amos comes out to greet us, probably having seen the dust our horses kicked up on the road. "Howdy, John. Billy." We dismount and tie up the horses, saying hellos and making small talk until we can talk proper. "I suspect you're here to ask about the girl. And the Wrights. Terrible thing," Amos says, looking away.

"Terrible ain't the half of it," I say, getting right to the point. "You notice anything strange when you were over there, Amos?"

His gaze shifts to Billy for an instant before he replies. "Kerosene," he says. "Weren't no accident, that fire."

Billy puffs out his chest, his face going red. "Now

why would you withhold that information from me, Amos?"

"Didn't seem right until there was an *official* lawman, Billy. Otherwise, it's just gossip."

I put a hand on Billy's shoulder. "Amos did the right thing. We can talk about it later. Anything else, Amos? Did you see anyone, or did Melanie say anything that might help? What about your boy?"

Before Amos can answer, the door opens and Noah steps out onto the porch. "That girl said 'twas the devil—"

"Get back in the house, boy!" Amos takes a threatening step toward his son.

"Amos, let him have his say."

"The boy's filled his head with nonsense, John—"

I silence him with a look. "Go ahead, son. What else did she say?"

The boy looks at his father warily, then says,

"Woe to those who call evil good, and good evil;
Who substitute darkness for light and light for darkness;
Who substitute bitter for sweet and sweet for bitter!"

Billy adds, "That's Isaiah 5:20."

"Did she say that?" I ask. "Or are you just praying?"

The boy shakes his head. "The girl said it, but I ain't

never gonna forget it. I ain't learned much Bible but the way she was when she came out of that fire..."

"Anything else?"

"Beware of false prophets, who come to you in sheep's clothing but inwardly are ravenous wolves," the boy says, his voice taking on an eerily adult tone.

"Get back inside, boy," Amos says, sounding disgusted. "'Fore I tan your hide." When the boy is gone, he says, "I 'pologize, John. Noah ain't much for brains but he can do the work of two men in the fields."

"His brains seemed fine rememberin' those verses," I say, "maybe you've got yourself a preacher in the making." Amos scoffs at that, but there's pride in his eyes just the same. "If you think of anything else, or your boy does, you tell me. Or tell Billy; he's as good as a lawman."

When they are out of earshot, Billy says, "Did you mean that, John? About me bein' a lawman?"

I tip my hat back on my head so Billy can see in my eyes that I'm not pulling his leg. "I meant it, all right. I mean to talk to Sheriff Toliver directly when we get back to town."

"Thanks, John, I mean, Deputy—"

"It's okay, Billy. You did good."

"Thanks, though, much obli—"

"Billy!" *Jesus fuck, what a day.*

Sheriff Toliver still isn't around, so I head back to Doc's to check on the girl, having sent Billy to talk to anyone who was at the sites of the previous fires. It would have been easier had there been any survivors, but...

"How's she doing?" Doc turns from the bed, a grim expression darkening his face.

"She's burning up, probably infection. It happens with extensive burns like these. I changed the dressing and applied more salve, but it's up to her body to fight."

Thank fuck Doc didn't say it was up to God. What kind of fucking god would let this happen in the first place? "Did she come out of it at all while I was gone?"

"She was pretty delirious between the pain and the fever. Rambled on with more Bible-sounding stuff. Something about recognizing good and evil." He shakes his head. "I wouldn't put too much stock in any of it, Johnny, she's in a bad way." Doc has this way of pinning a person with his eyes. I didn't want to look away. As he watches me, his face changes to a look of question. "What is it, Johnny? Did you find something out there?"

I clench my teeth. The more people who know

about the arson, the more likely that the person responsible will get wind of it. "This was no accident, Doc. Somebody burned down the Wrights' farm, I suspect to cover up the fact he killed them. Probably didn't realize the girl was there."

"There's another possibility," Doc says.

"Spit it out, Doc. No time for more mystery."

"There have been cases where the fire *is* the motive. The Wrights might have just been caught in it. There are theories that people have an affliction of sorts, or perhaps a moral deficiency, that makes them crave fire."

I start to grin. Doc isn't one for jokes, but surely this is his idea of pulling my leg.

Doc holds up his hands in surrender. "I'm not saying I buy into it, I'm saying it's a theory. There are cases of people who set houses afire, or even fields, just to watch them burn."

Doc is always reading up on the latest medicines and using fancy words while I spend my days throwing people in jail and breaking up fights. Most nights I spend at the saloon—which is exactly where I aim to go once I leave Doc's. What would it have been like if we'd started farming like we dreamed? I push the thought away. "I'll be over at the Last Chance. Send someone to get me when she comes around?"

Doc nods, returning to the girl's side. Something is

different about this one. He has a steely look in his eyes, challenging anyone—even death itself—to try to inflict any more harm on her. I respect the hell out of him.

I leave my horse at Doc's, knowing I'll be back there soon enough, and walk the dusty road toward the Last Chance. I watch the goings-on around me with a careful eye. *Could one of these folks be murdering people and burning down farmhouses to cover their tracks?* As much as I don't want to believe it, I know it might be the case. I think what Doc said about people craving fire and a thought occurs to me. I cross the street, taking a detour before quenching my thirst with a whiskey.

The Blacksmith shop stinks of heated metal and smoke. I call out to Seth Pollon, the smitty, but he is busy hammering away at a shoe and doesn't hear. Pollon has only been in town for a year or so. He'd apprenticed with old Calvin Ayers until recently. Calvin headed north to Colorado, where the air is supposed to be better for his ailing lungs. Seth just keeps pounding away, sweat pouring off his skin, until he gets the feeling he's being watched. He turns, startled to see me, but recovers quickly. "Be done soon."

I look around the shop, taking in the collection of tools with a new perspective. There are any number of potential weapons in Seth's arsenal. Not that he needs a weapon—he stands half a head taller than most men in town, and has the heavily-muscled body of a man accustomed to hard work.

Seth saunters over with his casual ease and boyish grin. I immediately feel the fool for even coming in here. Doc's stories of fire-loving ghouls have my thoughts all askew.

"What can I do for you, Deputy?" Seth says, looking over my head toward the road. "Your horse throw a shoe?"

"Oh, no. Nothing like that. I wanted to let you know we might have some trouble brewing." Seth's face turns hard and I plunge ahead before he can start asking questions. "Fire out at the Wrights, sorry to say it killed both Samuel and Ida." Seth's face changes again, to a countenance of pure sadness. "They had kin, a niece, staying with them. She survived, but she's over at Doc's in pretty bad shape."

"That's about the saddest thing I ever heard," Seth says genuinely, his deep voice almost cracking. "What kind of trouble are you expecting?"

I step closer, looking over my shoulder and speaking in a conspiratorial whisper. "We think the fire may have been set on purpose. If so, the one that done it might come looking for the girl, you know, in case she saw him." Seth seems to grow before my eyes and such a fierce anger crosses his face that I back up a step. "Doc can't stay with her 'round the clock and I don't have the men to stand guard either. Can I count on you to help if we need you?"

Seth straightens to his full height. It's like watching a mountain grow out of the landscape. "Just say the word, Deputy. Ain't nobody gonna even look at the girl funny while she's in my care."

I nod gravely and extends my hand to shake. I regret it immediately when Seth's giant paw swallows my hand and near grinds my bones to dust. "I'll stop by later. And thank you." I scurry away, needing that whiskey now more than ever.

The sound of raised voices from down the street catches my attention as I leave Seth's. I look longingly at The Last Chance, but my sense of duty won't allow me to ignore the angry shouts. *Never gonna get me that whiskey*. I sigh heavily, and begin walking toward the commotion.

I round the corner toward the Bar Z Corral and see the source of the ruckus. An angry mob is gathered around one of the big ironwood trees next to the corral.

That means someone is about to get strung up. I break into a run as the shouts grow louder and angrier. When I reach the mob, I shove my way through, finally pulling my revolver and firing a shot into the air.

All heads turn and people part when they see me. I shoulder past the last of the mob and get to the small clearing under the ironwood. Sure enough, a heavy rope is looped around one of the sturdy branches. I can't help but notice all the bald spots on the branch where the bark had been burned off by previous events like this one. Standing under the branch with the noose around his neck is Andy Onefeather, a half-breed Navajo who helps out at the Bar Z.

"What the hell is going on?" I say, still holding my pistol.

Ray Maxwell steps forward, towering over me. He is a bear of a man, tall and thick. Years of working his farm has made his body strong but it's growing up under the thumb of his father that has made him a hard man. Thomas Maxwell isn't one to spare the rod, and that goes for his sons, daughters, and his wife alike. Ray is the oldest and has always tried to protect his younger siblings, taking the brunt of his father's whiskey-fueled rage.

"We heard what happened out at the Wrights'

farm," Maxwell says in his slow drawl. "Justice needs to be done. An eye for an eye, and all that."

I look at Andy's terror-stricken face. "And what gives you the right to deal out justice? Furthermore, why do you think Andy had anything to do with it?"

Maxwell steps closer, practically bumping me. "Onefeather's been caught setting fires before, Deputy, you know that as well as I do. 'Sides," he adds, "it's in their blood. And as far as the right to deal out justice, well, somebody's gotta do it."

"That fire was an accident, Maxwell. Andy was trying to help put it out." I shake my head. "This has gone far enough." I poke a finger into Maxwell's chest. "Take the rope off him. Now." I turn to face the grumbling crowd. "Go on about your business, ain't gonna be no hangin's today—"

The blow sends me to my knees, and I drop the gun. Stars explode in my head in a dazzling array of colors. I go down on hands and knees, struggling to hold onto consciousness. Rough hands grab my shoulders and shove me the rest of the way to the ground. I breathe in a mouthful of dust and begin to cough, sending fresh pain into my chest and another round of stars across my vision. "Ray Maxwell," I manage, "you're under arrest."

Maxwell utters a barking laugh and says, "Let's finish this, boys."

I get the coughing under control and close my eyes until the dizziness clears. I struggle back to my hands and knees, searching the ground around me for the gun. The cries and cheers begin again, and I see a few other farmhands—Maxwell's bootlickers—begin to pull the rope, first getting out all the slack then starting to raise Andy Onefeather off the ground. "Stop this now, Maxwell, or you and your boys will be the next ones to swing."

"Don't think so, Deputy. Not as long as Toliver is sheriff."

I don't know what Maxwell means and don't have time to figure it out. I spot my gun in the dirt to my right and lunge for it. I roll onto my back and fire two quick shots at the men holding the rope. The first bullet explodes one of the men's knees, sending blood and bone chips raining down. The second slug catches him in the throat. A waterfall of black-red blood gushes from the wound, soaking the man's shirt. He lets go of the rope and slaps both hands to the gaping maw that used to be his neck. It is useless: blood squirts in every direction through his fingers. Then he is on the ground, twitching.

A booted foot stomps down on my wrist before I can swing my aim to the other hand—the one still holding the rope. Maxwell steps over the dying man to help the other ranch-hand hold the rope that holds the hanging Indian. Andy's turning purple and his eyes are bulging to the point where they might pop right out of his head.

I shift my gaze to the man stepping on my wrist. Jacob Vance glares down at me, then looks hungrily the hanging man.

I pull a knife from my belt and plunge it into the soft flesh behind Vance's knee. It goes in easy, as if it was going into warm butter. He screams and his legs buckle. I grab the pistol in my right hand, the wrist already swelling, and scramble to my feet. Stepping forward, I fire at the ranch-hand. The bullets take him high in the chest, sending him dancing backward in a shower of blood. Maxwell lets go of the rope - sending Andy's limp body to the dirt - and moves toward me, but I'm fast with the knife. I slash at Maxwell's throat and for a panicked second, I think I've missed. Then a gruesome red smile appears there, followed by a red geyser. I whirl and level the gun at the mob before Maxwell hits the ground. Only two shots left. "Back up! This is over unless someone else wants a piece of lead in 'em." The confused faces in the crowd turn to each other. They look sad, their bloodlust unsatiated. But none move on me. "Go on, now. And someone fetch Doc."

All eyes turn when I enter the Last Chance. They always do when a man wearing a badge steps in. The whispering comes next, followed by a few forced greetings. It's an odd thing: I can walk into the general store or the livery or the post office, and nobody bats an eye. But when I step into the saloon, everyone gets skittish. Maybe they've got some burden of guilt weighing on them that they think I know about. I recognize a few from the ugly scene at the Bar Z and know that's the case for them.

"Whiskey and a beer," I say, nodding to Spirit, who floats down the bar to pour the drinks. Shit, he even moves like a ghost.

I throw back the shot, imagining the whiskey is cleansing me as it goes down. Death always makes a man feel dirty, especially death by murder. But it's the little girl that is heavy on my mind. What kind of life is she going to have if she survives, looking like that? It might be a blessing if she doesn't make it. All burnt up, no kin left, haunted by whatever it was she'd seen—

"Why, it's Deputy John Pierce, bless my soul!"

I turn to the voice, already knowing who it belongs

to. Jim-Jim is the simple-minded nephew of Calvin Ayers, the former smitty. He does odd jobs around town, mucking out stalls, sweeping the floors, that sort of thing. Mostly he hangs around the Last Chance, wiping off tables, cleaning puke, and emptying spittoons—whatever Spirit can think of to keep him from bothering the customers.

"Howdy, Jim-Jim," I say, "how goes it?" Jim-Jim can be annoying as all hell if you're in a mood, but sometimes his dimwitted innocence is just the ticket.

"Oh, it goes, Deputy John Pierce, it surely does. Bless my soul."

I tip my beer, feeling good for the first time all day. "Then you better catch it before it gets away." It is an old saw between us, but one that never fails to bust Jim-Jim up good. He leans over and slaps his knees, braying that dumb laugh of his, and it just about makes me forget the sorrowful day I'm having.

Maxwell and his two henchmen are dead. Vance, the guy that mangled my wrist, is cooling off in one of the cells. Walking without a limp isn't part of his future.

Doc had tended to Andy Onefeather first. He'll live, but until he comes to, Doc isn't sure if he'll be right in the head. Something about being hanged like that can do something to a man's brain. Doc had tried to explain it, but my mind wandered.

The batwing doors fly open, sending a spear of sunlight across the barroom. The sheriff steps into the Last Chance, scanning the dimly-lit room, finally landing on his target: me. He saunters over, keeping his eyes fixed, until he stands almost close enough to kiss. “A word, Deputy,” he says through tight lips, then spins on his heel and leaves the bar. The buzz in the room, which had ceased when Toliver made his entrance, resumes at twice the volume, all eyes now on me.

“Are you in trouble, Deputy John Pierce?” Jim-Jim’s eyes are comically wide.

“Nah, Sheriff’s just having a bad day.” I finish my beer in three long swallows, nod to Jim-Jim and Spirit, and follow the sheriff. The sunlight is blinding after the gloomy interior of the saloon. Toliver is walking with purpose and is already back at his office. He opens the door and steps in without looking back. He knows his well-trained mutt will be right behind him. I dutifully pick up my pace and am relieved to get back to the office and out of the hellacious sun.

“Sheriff?” Toliver is already seated behind his desk, scowling at something. He raises his eyes over the paper he is holding and gives me a hard look. It is intended to wither me, I reckon, but I’ve been Toliver’s deputy long enough that it no longer works that way.

“You’ve had yourself quite a day, haven’t you,

Deputy Pierce?" Toliver's face is hard to read, but *happy* is definitely not among the choices that come to mind.

Word travels fast, I think, unsure if Toliver is referring to the attempted lynching or the fire at the Wrights'. "Just another day in Sundown," I say, hoping to assuage the sour mood Toliver looks to be in.

"I don't give a shit about those useless Maxwell boys. What the hell happened out at Wrights' farm?" Toliver snaps.

I choose my words carefully before answering. "Me and Billy went out to the scene. Whole place stunk of kerosene. That fire was no accident, Sheriff. Witness says they were killed before the fire." Toliver flinches, getting to his feet.

"What witness?"

"Little girl, kin of the Wrights that was staying with them."

He seems to ponder this, then nods. "Okay, okay," he says, pacing, "Who was it that set the fire? Did the killings?"

"We don't know yet, Sheriff. The girl was in a bad way. Doc had to give her something. Knocked her out. We'll get a description when she comes around." Toliver stops his pacing and runs a hand through his hair. "*If* she comes around," I add.

Toliver lets out a sigh and leans on the edge of his

desk, his eyes clear but full of worry. "You know what this means, Deputy?"

"Yeah. Billy and me already talked about it. The other fires..."

"The other fires," he echoes.

"I sent Billy off to talk to anyone who was nearby when the other fires happened. Ask 'em if they remember smelling kerosene. It's possible those were accidents, but given what the girl said—"

Toliver's head jerks up. "I thought she was out? What did she say?"

I grimace, hating to have to utter the next words. "That the devil killed them." Toliver opens his mouth, probably to tear into me, maybe ask if Santa Claus was a suspect as well, but I silence him with a raised hand. "I know it wasn't the devil, Sheriff, I just meant that she saw *someone*. She was babbling a bunch of nonsense, Bible verses and such."

Toliver nods. "Right. Okay. When will the girl be able to answer questions, did Doc say?"

I shrug. "He said she might be out a while. I'm heading back over there now." Toliver moves to the window to stare out at the street, looking for who-knows-what. He doesn't say anything more, so I start toward Doc's. Just as I approach, someone calls my name. Billy is riding toward me, waving like a lunatic. Good or bad news, I can't be sure. The street is quiet other than the frantic hoofbeats of Billy's horse. My gaze passes by the sheriff's office, and I spy Toliver still standing at the window, looking out.

Billy jumps off his horse, breathless, and tosses the reins sloppily over the hitching post. "It's for sure, John, the—"

I hold up a hand to silence the kid. "Whoa there, Billy. No need for the whole town to hear your news. Tie up your fucking horse proper, and meet me in Doc's."

"She's coming around, Johnny, good timing." Doc says.

Billy crashes through the door before I can respond.

"Heavens, Billy!" Doc cries, "Where's the fi—" He stops himself, realizing that the expression doesn't fit the situation too well.

"Sorry, Doc," Billy breathes, "but I need to update John—"

I hold up a hand again and Billy's mouth snaps shut. He is obedient if nothing else. "Settle down, son. Doc says the girl's stirring. Hold your tongue until I talk to her." I start toward the back room that Doc uses for patients. "Just me, Billy," I tell him, "No need to overwhelm the poor thing."

"Should I fetch the sheriff?" Billy asks.

"Not yet. Let's see if we can't piece this fucking mess together and deliver it to Toliver with a bow on it."

When I step into the back room, the girl is moaning and thrashing around on the bed. I watch her for a spell, debating on calling for the doc, then her eyes flutter open and she looks around, confused. "It's okay, you're at Doc's and he's taking good care of you."

Her eyes find me and seem to focus on me, clearing up a bit. "Doc?" Her voice is all scratchy, probably dried out from the fire or being out for a while. I move next to the bed and pour her a glass of water from the pitcher Doc keeps there. I hold the glass to her lips, no easy feat given the bulky bandages that cover her face with just cutouts for her eyes, nose, and mouth. She nods to let me know she's finished. "Thank you," she says. I blink, amazed at how much better her voice sounds. Kids are so damned resilient. Unless it's the cholera. Voices from the other room grow louder but I ignore them, focused on getting some answers if I can.

"I'm very sorry for what happened," I say gently. Her eyes widen, a horrifying sight given the way they are sunken behind those bandages. Then her chest starts heaving as she tries to suck in enough air. Maybe she'd forgotten everything until I went and reminded her. She starts thrashing around and I grab her shoulders to try to settle her, but there is a gap in the bandages and my hands land on bare skin. I feel them slip and see great patches of flesh sliding off her, leaving a raw, red mess. I pull back with a cry, watching in horror as blood and pus ooze, soaking the bandages. Then she starts screaming.

Doc is there in a flash, administering a shot. I step back, staring at my hands. Those traitorous hands that had inflicted pain on the poor girl. I'm thinking, of course, about a different little girl. Melanie calms down almost immediately, and her eyes slip shut. I look around. Billy and the sheriff are staring at me. "I...I didn't..."

"Go on, out of here, all of you." Doc's voice holds no room for discussion. Billy leads me out as Doc starts applying salve to the new wounds.

"What the hell was that?" Toliver barks when we reach the outer room.

"I just—"

"Never mind," Toliver snaps. "Billy, take him over to the Last Chance and get him straight. I'll handle questioning the girl, Pierce."

I nod without looking back, and the next thing I know, I'm standing at the bar and Spirit is asking me if he wants a refill. I look down at the whiskey glass in his hand and shake my head. I need to stay sober. Stay focused.

"What happened in there, John?" Billy's voice is gentle, but his eyes are wide in that crazy way of his.

"I don't rightly know, Billy. She seemed okay, then..." I shrug. Maybe I should've taken that refill after all.

"Doc'll fix her up," Billy says, looking down at his feet.

"What'd you find out about the other fires, Billy?"

Billy's eyes fill with excitement. He'd forgotten about the news he'd so badly wanted to deliver before we went to Doc's. "I found folks that helped put out a couple of the other fires—the one at Harrisons' and the one at Miltons'—both remembered smelling kerosene."

I nod, wondering if they remembered it before or after Billy had mentioned it. I pose the question to Billy.

Billy looks hurt and starts to say something, but it is drowned out by loud shouts from across the bar. I glance across the crowded room, not overly concerned, but my hand moves on its own to the butt of my pistol. Whiskey is the match that lights a lot of angry fuses. So long as lead doesn't start flying, I'm inclined to let the boys work it out on their own. I crane my neck and when I see who is involved in the ruckus, my hand tightens on the sandalwood pistol grip. "Let's go, Billy."

Bloody fucking hell, will this day ever end?

The knife feels heavy in his hand, but it's a good weight. It is strength. It is destiny. It is the shadow's savior. The room is quiet save for the raucous snores of the sleeping man. The shadow looks down at him, knowing he should feel sadness for what is about to be. About to *become.* But he can't summon it. He feels only hope and comfort. Safety. The sounds of violence from the Last Chance rise above the normal night-time sounds of horses chuffing and the occasional footsteps on the hard plank of the boardwalk. The ruckus brings a smile to his face but does nothing to sate the screams. No, distant pain will not offer succor for what ails him. He looks at the knife and nods. "Yes," he whispers. "Yes."

The man stirs. Could he be such a light sleeper that the shadow's susurrate words have woken him? His open, bulging eyes answer the question. "Ike?" His voice is filled with the confusion brought on by a sudden awakening from the deepest slumber.

"The very one," the shadow answers with a smile. He feels no need for the mask this night. This is less about silencing the demons, more to protect himself. *Still, he could be the one.*

The man tries to sit up but the shadow places a hand on his chest. "Be still."

Now he sees the knife and he's fully awake, alert. Men in his profession must be accustomed to this. Being dragged out of a good night's sleep by the call of duty.

The shadow smiles, drawing a confused look from the man in the bed. *This is no call of duty,* the shadow thinks. No, it is the call of some higher power. Some ancient prophecy, perhaps. Fate isn't for the faint of heart.

"Ike, whatever you think—"

The shadow moves fast, the knife an extension of his hand, of his *being*. The man's ear drops to the pillow followed by a gush of blood. His face registers shock, knowing something has happened, then the pain hits and he opens his mouth to scream. But the shadow is faster. He clamps a hand over the man's mouth, muffling his cry and reducing it to a mere moan. His eyes are wild now, the knowledge that his end has drawn nigh settling on him like a cold fog. A desperate hand clutches the shadow's, but another flash of the blade loosens it. He has cut the man deep enough—rupturing both veins and tendons—to render that hand useless. The man realizes his error, and when his other hand snakes out from beneath his blankets, he tries for the shadow's face. Alas, the shadow is faster again. The shadow is *always* faster. The blade sinks deep into the man's armpit, eliciting another strangled moan. The panic in his eyes is pure, now. This is no simple fear, no conscious decision to be afraid of the specter that has appeared like a nightmare. No, this is stark-white terror, bringing out the primal instinct to survive that lies dormant in most men. He is bucking like a rodeo bull, squirming like a rattler caught under the pitchfork's tine. But with only two crippled hands to work with, his doom is nearly upon him. It is up to the shadow—it has always been up to him, him and the blade—how many more breaths he draws.

He presses the tip of the blade to the man's gut, low on his belly. The man stops thrashing, knowing it will only serve to drive the blade deeper. Tears spill from his eyes. This is resignation. He is beaten. The shadow leans in close, smelling the metallic odor of blood that leaks from the gaping hole where the man's ear was moments earlier, and wonders idly if the man can hear anything from it. He moves the blade, sliding the tip into the man's left nostril. Before he understands what is going to happen, the shadow flicks his wrist, flaying the man's nose like a trout. He does the second nostril with a deft movement, and the blood pours evenly down both cheeks. The man's eyes bulge, making the shadow's next target an easy choice.

The shadow laughs as the blade slides easily into the soft pouch of skin under one eye, encountering no resistance. Leaning closer, he moves the knife in a circular motion, ignoring the incessant moans and the snot and blood that are defiling the hand that remains pressed to the man's mouth. He'll have to take it away soon. There is no longer a secondary way for the man to draw breath.

First, he finishes his work on the eye. It hangs loosely on the cheek, only a pulpy umbilical of veins or nerves holding it in place. The shadow marvels that the pupil still moves and wonders if it still *sees*—but his curiosity is short-lived, the need to let the blade do its work too great. He slices the anchoring tissue and watches the eyeball roll down the man's cheek, bounce on the bed, and disappear with a wet splat to the floor.

The man in the bed is still now. Pain and shock have shut his mind down, rendering his body useless. It belongs to the shadow—no, it belongs to the blade. He lets the blade guide him, following the course it takes his hand. He's curious as the blade shows him the man's insides. The same coils of ropy guts that he'd seen at the Wrights'. Did he think it would look any different because he is a man of science? He realizes with some humor that he did. He doesn't know exactly why he thought a doctor's guts would differ from those of a farmer.

He takes a step back some time later and admires the work of the blade. Doc is unrecognizable as a person. His handiwork—his artwork—looks like someone tried to dress a deer on his bed. His skin is laid open from head-to-toe, muscle and bone and most of the organs visible. The shadow rotates his arm, realizing it will be sore tomorrow from the work it has done. Next, he realizes how clear his head is and knows an achy arm is a small price to pay. The screams are gone, silent. At least for now.

Even though he has no need to cover up the blade's work as he has in the past, the night's work is not complete. There's still the girl. With Seth Pollon standing guard, getting to her will be no easy trick. With his head clear, there is no *need* to use the blade—or let the blade use him—but with the screams, what choice does he have? The thought of being captured, jailed, with no way to silence the screams, is terrifying. He'd rather hang, or get shot trying to get the girl. With a final look at the doc's pulpy remains, he turns to face the night.

I SHOVE MY WAY THROUGH THE CROWD UNTIL I reach the far corner where the confrontation is heating up. The corner table is unofficially reserved for poker games. I can't remember a time I'd come into the Last Chance, regardless of the hour, and there wasn't a game going on. Sometimes there are only two or three people, usually five or six. Tonight, the table is full. Eight men surround the mess of cards, and in the center sits the biggest pot I can remember seeing.

Most of the chairs are tipped over, probably the result of the men jumping to their feet when the hoopla began. Frank Delaney brandishes a deadly-looking knife, the gleam of the blade matching the fierce sparkle of rage in his eyes. Boone Wilson stands facing him, a two-shot derringer aimed to gut-shoot him. Boone's expression is a spooky mix of eerie calm and delirious anticipation. I don't like the odds of this ending without a killing or two. Boone had come to town just a year or so ago and had quickly gained a reputation for being both a card sharp and a hardcase. He'll never back down.

"Boone," I say evenly, "I'm not in the mood for

cleaning up any more blood or dragging your ass to jail. So put down—"

"You ever see a deck of cards with five aces, Deputy?" His tone matches the calm side of his expression, but that can change with the twitch of a finger.

"I told you, Wilson," Delaney bellows, his voice thick with either emotion or booze, or both, "I played the cards I was dealt."

I catch Billy's eyes and shift mine toward Delaney, signaling Billy to creep over that way. Billy gives me the slightest of nods and this is enough for me. I turn to Boone. "What'd you have?"

Boone's gaze flicks toward the table. "Queen high flush," he says. "Hearts."

I note the five cards splayed near Boone. "What about you, Frank?"

"Full house, aces over fours."

I again scan the table, seeing Delaney's hand. "Who dealt?"

"I did, Deputy," a voice calls. I find the speaker and realize with a sinking feeling it's Arthur West. Delaney and West are often drinking together and, just as often, losing at cards together. They both work on and off at a few of the ranches when there is work. They take shifts in the mines when there isn't planting or harvesting to be done. Are West and Delaney sly enough to pull off a card cheat?

"August," I say, picking out the tall figure from the crowd, "gather up the cards for me. Let's get to the bottom of this." I wait as August Paulson shoves his way forward to the table. He makes sure to stay out of the crossfire of Delaney and Wilson. I also spot that Billy has made his way around the crowd and is just a few feet from Delaney.

I motion to August. "Start laying them face up by number. Pay special attention to the aces, if you please."

August Paulson runs the Sundown newspaper but could have done just about any job he chose. He is as tall and lanky as he is smart, but there is tight, ropy muscle on those bones. I picked him not for those reasons, though. I know August is beholden to nobody because of his role. He has a reputation for telling it like it is, in his little paper. Just the cold facts, with no concern for how the news impacts anyone.

I watch Delaney and West as August scoops up the cards in his big hands. Beads of sweat pop on Delaney's forehead and West's eyes are fixed on Delaney. I have no doubt how this is going to play out, and am glad Delaney only has a knife. West's eyes narrow and I follow his gaze. He's picked up on Billy's movements. Before I can draw, West pulls out his six-shooter and has the barrel snug against the back of Boone's skull.

"Back off, Billy," West says, his voice just a little south of steady. "Drop that pea-shooter on the table, Boone. Not asking you twice."

Billy spreads his hands and takes a half-step back. Boone keeps the derringer aimed at Delaney's gut, a smirk pulling at the corners of his lips. *Oh, shit, here we go.*

"Boone," I say, "you pull that trigger and you don't even get the pleasure of seeing Delaney bleed out. Your brains'll be all over the table. Let's get out of this without any killin' and sort it out later. Live to fight another day and all that."

Boone's eyes flick to me, his smirk turning into a grin. "Sage advice, Deputy Pierce," he says. "West, don't you flinch on me, I'm putting the gun on the table, all right?"

West doesn't say a word, but I don't fancy the look on his face. I figure it's about even odds West pulls the trigger anyway.

Boone lowers the derringer and places it on the table. West keeps his gun pressed against the man's skull. "Frank," West says, "gather up your winnings." Frank starts scooping up the money and stuffing it into his pockets. When he reaches for the money around the table that wasn't in the pot, West says, "No, Frank. We ain't stealing. Take what's in the pot and that's all. Fair and square."

Boone scoffs and I'm sure West is going to pull the trigger. Instead, he twirls the gun so he holds it by the barrel and clubs Boone over the head. Boone slumps to the floor. Just as quick, West twirls the gun back so his finger is on the trigger. His eyes are everywhere at once, looking for anyone that might want to play the hero. West is fast, I know, and I'm glad to see nobody pulled. Delaney grabs Boone's derringer.

West nods. "Pierce, Billy, put your pieces on the table. Real slow."

"I'm not doing that, Arthur. I haven't pulled and I'm not planning on it. You want to add killing a deputy in cold blood to your list of mistakes, that's on you." West stares at me, his eyes a mix of fear and something that looks like madness. I think for a second I might have played it wrong, then Delaney speaks.

"Let's go, Art," he says, "like you said, fair and square."

The bulging of West's eyes seems to occur a split-second before the gunshot echoes through the Last Chance. West looks down. A small hole in his shirt begins to leak dark blood. He places a hand over the wound, and this small pressure does the opposite of his intent. Blood, more black than red, spurts between his fingers copiously. He looks up, confused. A second shot erases that look. His cheek explodes in torn flesh and glistening white chunks of teeth and bone. Without a sound, he keels over next to Boone.

Delaney looks around wildly, waving the stupid derringer this way and that. I draw, smooth as a silk handkerchief, and put a bullet in Delaney's gun hand. Delaney squeals like a schoolgirl, dropping the derringer. Billy moves quickly, using the butt of his pistol on Delaney's head.

"All right, excitement's over, folks." I find August easily. "Go fetch the sheriff and Doc." August turns and ambles through the crowd as calmly as if he is going to get a drink at the bar. The man is cool, should have been a law man. "Okay," I say, "who dispatched Mr. West? Step up, come on now."

The crowd parts and I can't help but grin. Rosie May, one of the saloon whores, stands defiantly, then raises her skirt and slips the revolver into a thigh holster. I don't mind the generous amount of leg she shows in the process. Not that I haven't seen it before.

I've been with Rosie, first as a customer when the loneliness got to be too much, then later as a friend. It occurs to me now—at the damn strangest of times—that I have real feelings for her.

"That limp dick owed me money," she says flatly.

ME AND BILLY COVER UP WEST'S BODY. *ISN'T anything Doc can do for this one.* I wrap a towel around Delaney's hand, noting it is a couple fingers shy. Delaney is crying and moaning so Spirit gives him shots of rot gut whiskey until he shuts up. Boone comes to and is looking no worse for wear. Billy gathers the cards from the table and lays them out. Sure enough, there is an extra ace of spades. I rip Delaney's sleeves up. There's a clever little contraption that holds a few more aces. "Son of a bitch."

"Deputy Pierce," August calls. "Nobody at the sheriff's." But it's his next words that chill me. "Seth's gone to fetch Doc."

"Who's with the girl?" August only stares dumbly at me. I leap at him, grabbing a fistful of shirt and pulling him close. "Who's with the girl?" I get no answer and push the man away. "Billy!" He's already next to me. "Let's go."

We run out of the saloon and across the street toward Doc's. I spot a man at the door and holler, "You there! Stop!" I had drawn when I first spotted the figure —Seth, I can now tell—holding a pistol. "Drop it, Seth," I say, remembering Doc's theory about people who like fire. Remembering Seth at the forge hammering away.

"Deputy, thank God," he says, lowering his weapon. "Doc's dead, someone killed him."

The door to Doc's office creaks open. Me and Seth both swing our weapons toward the sound. Sheriff Toliver stands silhouetted in the lantern light. "Pierce, how could you leave the girl unattended?"

Christ, I think, holstering my pistol. *What a fucking mess.* "Sheriff, is she all right?"

"No thanks to you," Toliver grumbles, and turns back inside.

Seth slides his weapon into its holster. "I'm real sorry, John," he says, "when August said there'd been a shootin' I figured you'd got the one that was a threat to her."

It makes sense, I realize. "It's okay, Seth. All's well with her, it seems. Billy, go check on the doc." Billy takes off at a run as me and Seth follow the sheriff into Doc's office.

I quickly bring Toliver up to speed about the goings-on at the Last Chance, and Seth tells his story about what he found at Doc's.

August steps in, frowning.

"Sheriff Toliver," he says, "I couldn't find you at your office and I was beginning to worry."

Billy shoves past August, pale and shaking. "Doc's d-dead. Not just dead," he says. I catch a whiff of his breath—he's puked. "He's all c-cut up..." Billy turns and leans out the door, retching.

August ignores Billy. "Sheriff, you weren't here when I came to fetch Doc..." He looks up and down the street, his face a mask of confusion.

The sound that comes from within the room starts as a low moan but quickly rises to a banshee's scream. I shoulder past Toliver and kneel beside the bed. "It's all right," I coo, "you're all right. You're safe."

The girl's eyes go wide and she sits up in bed, arm straight, index finger pointing, "Devil!" Then her eyes roll back into her head and she collapses back on the bed, trembling.

I turn in time to see Sheriff Toliver grab Seth and spin him roughly against the wall. "I'm arresting you for the murder of Doc James," he says, pulling Seth's gun and tossing it to the floor behind him. *Doc James*, how could I forget?

August steps back. "Sheriff—"

"Disperse, Mr. Paulson, you'll get your story but we've got work to do here."

August glances helplessly at me, his eyes pleading.

But there's something else. They look wary. The events of the day flash through my mind. I get silently to my feet, slipping my gun out of its well-oiled holster like a whisper. I raise it slowly before I speak. "Step back."

Billy gawks from the doorway, wiping his mouth. August is nodding slowly, his eyes still on the sheriff. Toliver turns, eyes narrowing. "I've got him, John. Holster that fucking thing."

"Step back, Toliver," I say, "just until we get this sorted out."

Toliver's eyes widen, somehow hardening, his face blazing with fury. Through gritted teeth, he says, "What are you doing, John?"

I hold his gaze. "Where were you, Sheriff?"

"I don't have to explain my whereabouts to anyone. 'Specially you, *Deputy*."

Something clicks in my head. "Billy, the first time I talked to the girl, when did you and Sheriff Toliver come into the room?"

Billy looks at him, dazed, still thinking about Doc, I figure. "Right before she started going all crazy..."

I nod. "Toliver—" The sheriff moves fast, grabbing Billy and using him as a shield, producing a knife from somewhere and holding it to his throat, the blade pressing hard into the tender flesh. A thin line of blood runs down Billy's neck.

"I reckon you ought to lower that pistol, Pierce," Toliver says, dragging Billy toward the bed.

"I can't do that. Put the knife away, Toliver, or we both know how this ends."

Toliver grins, an evil, menacing thing, and I ponder how I'd never seen the madness in his eyes before. "August," he says, keeping his eyes on me, "I need you and Seth to leave. Go home. Close the door on your way out."

"Ike," I say, "we can do this without any more killing."

Toliver presses the blade harder, issuing a steady stream of blood leaking down Billy's neck. His shirt is soaking it up. Billy gasps and utters a low moan.

"Not gonna tell you again," Toliver says.

I nod, and Seth and August back out of the room, closing the door as they exit. "Now what, Ike? You just let two witnesses walk out the door. Why not put the knife down, okay?"

"I am the knife, John. Don't you see?"

I swallow past the lump. I know how to deal with the roughest, toughest hardcases that come to Sundown, but this? I have no idea how to rectify this. "I reckon I don't see, Ike."

"It's the screams, John, the hellish screams. The

knife...I...we need to quiet the screams. They're starting again, John. I-I can't take it."

I recall Melanie's words that Noah quoted:

Woe to those who call evil good, and good evil,

Who substitute darkness for light and light for darkness;

Who substitute bitter for sweet and sweet for bitter.

Beware of false prophets, who come to you in sheep's clothing but inwardly are ravenous wolves.

Even something Maxwell said about Toliver is starting to make sense. "Ike, there has to be a way to make the screams stop without killing. It's Billy, Ike. You can't...you can't kill him just like that."

Toliver winces. "It ain't like that, John. It's like...like taking medicine—"

The girl moves with a roar, grabbing the scalpel from the table in one smooth motion and lunging at Toliver, driving the blade into his throat. Toliver drops the knife and his grip on Billy loosens. Billy pulls away, sprawling to the floor. I stand riveted as the girl goes to work. She looks feral, teeth bared, eyes wild, as she plunges and hacks. Blood is everywhere and parts of Toliver that only Doc could've identified are hanging out of the open wound. Air wheezes in and out—not though his mouth but through the gaping hole in his windpipe. He finally goes down, his throat a grisly mess. The girl falls back on the bed, soaked in blood, weeping.

Billy stares, holding a hand to the small slice on his own throat. "Go fetch Seth and August," I say, my eyes still on the girl. Billy scrambles to his feet and leaves. When the door is shut, I step toward the bed. "I'm gonna need you to put down that blade," I say softly. "It's over. You killed the devil."

The girl looks at the scalpel she is still holding as if she's never seen it before. The look in her eyes—barely visible through the mask of Toliver's blood and, of course, the bandages—turns to disgust and she throws it on the floor. She wipes her hands on her nightshirt as if the blade had been dirty. Toliver's blood leaves angry red streaks on the white garment. I wonder what kind of marks this will leave on her soul.

I WAIT WITH BILLY FOR THE COACH TO ARRIVE. There is both a doctor and a sheriff supposed to be onboard, both from Tucson. At that point, I'll not only relinquish my title of acting sheriff, but I'll be through being a lawman altogether. I deputized Billy and will recommend to the new sheriff that it remains so. Then, I'll start farming my land like I'd planned before Nora and Charlotte died.

Me and Billy, with August's help, went over the list of fires that took place in the surrounding area. The newspaper has records going back further than either mine or Billy's memories, and we determined there to be at least sixteen fires that could have been Toliver's work. Seventy-three people had died in those fires. Or, I realize, were killed by Toliver's blade before the fires were set.

Andy Onefeather recovered with no lingering issues. Out of gratitude for saving him, Andy's enlisted a friend from the reservation who knows some medicine to help out until the new doc arrives. The man, called Sani, has done wonders with little Melanie using some concoction of plants and herbs to fight back the infection. I wish Doc was alive to see the Indians' way of making medicine.

Melanie is never going to be that pretty little girl, just like Billy said, but she is alive. Up and around, as a matter of fact, and talking a blue streak. She seems like she is going to be all right, against the odds.

I tried to locate Melanie's kin—August helped with that, too—and received only more bad news. The reason she was staying with the Wrights was because her parents had both died within a week of each other—her father from a rattlesnake bite and her mother from an overdose of laudanum. There appear to be no other living relatives, at least none we could track down. I decided to care for the girl myself until someone claims her. I don't reckon anybody will. In fact, I hope nobody does. The little girl needs someone who cares, and I need something to help mend my ailing heart. Being a deputy wasn't doing it, there's too much bad to be seen. If I hadn't already known that, the events of the past several weeks have shone a bright light on it.

"Yonder, she comes," Billy says, pulling me out of my thoughts.

I look at the dust rising in the distance. A sudden fear grips my heart. Something is going to foil my plans —an Indian attack on the coach before it arrives. Or when it does arrive, there'll be no lawman on board.

"You okay, boss?" Billy asks.

I turn to him, feeling as tired as I've ever felt. "Just pondering life," I say, enjoying Billy's befuddled look. "You sure you want to be a lawman?" Billy's face lights up and I know the answer before he speaks.

"It's what I've always wanted," he says, his voice unusually soft. "Ever since I was a kid." I have to hold back a laugh. Billy is *still* a kid as far as I'm concerned. He continues, "At least since my daddy was killed."

I study him. Billy is always a ball of energy, full of smiles and excitement. This somber side of him is new. Unexpected. "I never knew that, Billy."

He nods. "A gang of outlaws was terrorizing the area, raiding farms, robbing stagecoaches. Cowardly things that gangs do when they have the numbers and the firepower and the cover of night." Billy's eyes glisten with tears, but whatever he is seeing, it is far in the past. "They came to our place one night. We didn't have much but they took what we had. My daddy was a brave man but he was smart. He let them take what they wanted in order to keep his family safe. Until what they wanted was my ma."

"I'm sorry," I say, "I had no idea."

"He fought them as hard as a man can fight. But in the end, there was too many of them. They killed him and raped my ma. She was never the same after that. Hardly spoke. I took care of my little brother and sister. Ma died a couple years after from drinking whiskey and taking laudanum." His breath hitches and he wipes a hand across his face, then turns to me, his eyes cold steel. "I'll never forget them, John. Every one of their spineless, chicken-hearted faces is burned in my brain. I aim to find 'em."

Billy's words chill me. "Billy—"

"I aim to find 'em and arrest them all. I'll see them

hang, John, I swear it. It won't bring my folks back, but it's something, isn't it?"

I turn to watch the coach draw closer. I feel comfort in my decision to leave the lawing to men like Billy. Men with a passion for it. I put a hand on his shoulder and squeeze. "It is most definitely something, Billy. I'm proud of you."

Billy offers a shy smile then shifts his gaze to the coach, eager to see the new sheriff. I'm just as eager to meet the new doc and get him taking care of Melanie. Rosie May is watching her while I wait for the coach. She's taken a real shine to the little girl, and I wonder if there might be something there for the three of us.

The coach rolls to a stop in a cloud of dust as we stand. I still have my hand on Billy's shoulder. A tiny voice calls and I turn. Melanie and Rosie are coming to join us. I smile and wave. The coach driver jumps down and swings the side door open, and the future of Sundown steps into the blazing sun.

AFTER SUNDOWN

Tom Deady

I finish milking the cows and start toward the house for breakfast when I see dust rising in the distance. It's too early for visitors, the sun is barely up. I know right off there's trouble by the way my gut lurches, as if there's something in there trying to get out. I guess I still have some of my lawman instincts.

I rinse off my hands at the pump and stand on the porch. A single rider, by the looks of the dust being thrown, but still too far away to be sure. I grab my shotgun from inside the door, keeping an ear out to make sure Melanie and Rosie aren't up yet. The house is silent. I close the door and walk toward the gate.

The rider comes through Valle Seco and crests the hill. The big white hat tells me it's Billy Snow. Still holding the shotgun, my hands relax. Unlike my stomach. Whatever he's coming out to tell me is bad. The way he's pushing his horse tells me it's real bad. I walk back to the house to put on a pot of coffee.

Billy bursts in a few minutes later without knocking. His face is red and sweaty, and his eyes are wild. If my guts weren't all twisted up it might have been funny. "John," he says, his voice a couple octaves higher than normal, "I need your help."

"I didn't think you were out here at this hour to feed the chickens," I say, hoping to lighten the mood, but Billy doesn't seem to hear me. Once his mouth gets going, it sometimes leaves his brain behind.

"You gotta come to town. I'll deputize you to make it official—"

"Whoa," I say, holding up a hand to stop him. "Slow down, Billy." Whatever help he thinks he needs, I'm done being a lawman, and he knows better than to even ask.

His face contorts like he's in physical pain. "It's them, John. They killed Sheriff Armstrong and they'll be coming for me tonight."

I think for a second that I must have heard him wrong. But I know I didn't. Cold spreads through me as my mind tries to figure out who it is Billy is talking about. Sam Armstrong took over as sheriff in Sundown two years ago, replacing Ike Toliver. He is—*was* a good man and a good sheriff. But I don't know of any enemies, let alone enemies that would murder him and then come for Billy.

"Who did it, Billy? And why didn't you already arrest them?" He's shaking his head fast, wide-eyed and looking unhinged. I take him by the shoulders and sit him down at the table. "Relax," I tell him. It's a stupid thing to say, even for me. I pour us each a coffee and sit across from him. "Who did it?" I ask again. I keep my voice soft and easy.

"The ones that killed my daddy," he says. "One of 'em, anyway."

I remember my last day as deputy, waiting for Sheriff Armstrong to arrive on the coach. Billy had told me why he wanted to be a lawman. A gang of outlaws had murdered his father and raped his mother. He'd sworn that day he was going to bring them to justice. "You tracked 'em down," I say, finding it difficult to keep the shock out of my voice. Billy is a good deputy, but he'd been a little kid when his father was killed. I didn't think he'd ever really find them.

He takes a sip of coffee. His hands are shaking and that's when I truly understand how bad this is. Billy is young and impulsive. He talks too much and is too excitable. But he is usually fearless. Whoever killed Armstrong has the poor kid just about out of his mind with fear.

"I been looking for 'em since Armstrong showed up," Billy says. "He was helpin' me. Him and August."

I nod. August Paulson runs the Sundown newspaper and would have made a damn good deputy himself if he'd had a mind to. Armstrong had been a lawman in Dodge City and Santa Fe before coming to Sundown. I expect he'd telegrammed people back there to help Billy. August kept in regular contact with newsmen all across the country. I guess I shouldn't be surprised Billy tracked down the outlaws when he had that kind of help.

"I reckon they got word that I'd been askin' around and decided it'd be better if they found me before I found them."

It makes sense, but there's one thing I don't understand. "Why did they kill Armstrong?"

Billy shakes his head. "It was my fault, John. There was a brawl at the Last Chance. I had both cells doubled up and was tryin' to keep those drunks from killing each other. I told Sheriff Armstrong I'd take the overnight shift minding the jail if he'd stop by my place and feed Whitey."

Whitey was Billy's old coonhound and the kid treated it better than most men treated their wives. I can picture the rest in my head, but I let Billy tell it.

"They must have been waitin' there to ambush me. When Armstrong showed up, they thought it was me and... when he didn't show this morning to relieve me, I went by his house but he wasn't there. I went home to check on Whitey and that's when I found him."

"How do you know it was them?" I ask.

Billy runs a hand through his hair. "They left a message."

I hold out my hand. "Let me see it."

He has an expression I'll never forget. He looks like a man who's had a glimpse into Hell. "You'll have to go to my place to read it for yourself," he says. "It's written on my wall in Armstrong's blood."

I'd seen a lot of bad things in my time as a lawman. The worst turned out to be Sheriff Toliver. He'd murdered dozens of people in and around Sundown, getting away with it for the longest time because he covered up his killings by burning down his victims' houses. Fires aren't uncommon in the desert, so nobody suspected a thing. Until he left a witness behind.

That had been the worst I'd ever seen. Until now.

What Billy was talking about was something else. Toliver had had some sort of brain sickness that made him do what he did. This...this was evil.

When I think I can talk without my voice shaking, I ask, "What did it say, Billy?"

Billy closes his eyes. "It said, 'Your daddy died begging for his life. Your mother—" His voice breaks and he pauses to take a deep breath. "Your mother lived begging for more. Armstrong died with your name on his lips.'"

I stare at the kid, so many questions rattling around in my head. How much blood did it take to write all that? Why didn't they go after Billy last night? I stay silent, trying to think of something useful to say, when I hear footsteps behind me. I turn to see Melanie—the witness Toliver had left behind—rubbing sleep out of her eyes. She's flushed from sleep...or she's coming down with something.

She smiles when she sees our visitor. "Hi, Billy." She runs over and gives him a hug. Billy hugs her right back, clinging to her as though he might never let go.

Melanie had ended up helping solve the Toliver murders even though she'd been burned up pretty bad. What with her not having any kin, I decided to take her in as my own. *Our* own. I'd married Rosie May, a former saloon girl, and we made ourselves a nice home. We farm the land and have some dairy cows and chickens. It's good, honest work and we've carved out a nice life. We're a family, even if we didn't get there by the usual means.

Rosie walks in next. While she's happy to see Billy, she knows it's not a social visit. "Howdy, Billy," she says carefully.

"Howdy, Miss Rosie," he says, finally letting go of Melanie.

His eyes glisten and I'm not sure if it's from what happened to Armstrong or because of Melanie. He did take a shine to her, almost as powerful as I did, while we were keeping watch over her after the fire. It's a strange thing, the way she can bring such joy to a heart while breaking it a little at the same time. That fire might have taken away her beauty but it couldn't touch her spirit.

"There's been some trouble in Sundown," I say, and immediately regret it.

Melanie goes pale and tears spill. "The devil's come back," she says flatly.

She'd witnessed Toliver kill her aunt and uncle and had insisted he was the devil. Rosie and I had never asked her about it, figuring she'd talk to us when she was ready. If she could ever really be ready to talk about something like that. I cursed myself for my blunder.

"No, Melanie," I say calmly, "this is different. That bad man is dead, and he can never hurt you again."

She shakes her head and her eyes go blank, as if she's looking at something a hundred miles away that only she can see. "You can't kill the devil, Daddy," she says.

I don't answer. I don't know how to. So I turn to Rosie. "I need to go into town and take care of a few things," I say.

Before I can go on, Melanie leaps onto my lap and grabs me fiercely around the neck. Her face is buried in my chest and her words are muffled but I can still make them out. "Please don't go, Daddy."

I push her hair out of her eyes and feel the heat of her skin. I glance worriedly at Rosie.

"She's fine, John," Rosie says. "It's her burns acting up."

I nod and close my eyes, hating the choice I have to make. The choice I've already made. "I have to go, Melanie. Billy needs my help. There're some bad men that want to hurt him and I can't let that happen. You understand?"

She doesn't answer, just shakes her head.

I look at Rosie for help. Her face is tight, lips forming a thin line, but her eyes are resigned. She peels Melanie from my lap.

"Do you remember when Daddy helped catch the

bad man that hurt your aunt and uncle?" Melanie nods. "Well, now he has to go catch another bad man who is hurting people."

At this, tears slip down Melanie's cheeks.

"Thanks, Rosie," I say, giving her a hug. I give Melanie a kiss on the top of her head and go to fetch my gun belt.

I SIT IN THE SHERIFF'S OFFICE FEELING AS THOUGH the past two years were only a dream. Nothing in the office has changed. The same wanted posters hang there, the same piles of papers on the sheriff's desk. Even the smell is the same: a rancid mix of sweat, piss, puke, and old food. How had I ever managed to do this every day?

August sits across from me, studying me. His mildly amused expression tells me he knows what I'm thinking. Billy is pacing back and forth across the small room, boots tapping out a rhythm on the wood floor that is somehow calming and annoying at the same time.

"Billy?" He pauses to look at me. "You want to fill us in on what you know?"

He sighs, his face set hard. "I was hopin' Sani would have some news but he's probably..." Billy waves his hands around in the air. "He's probably doin' his magic or praying to the Great Spirit or whatever."

I try to cover up my smile. Even in the direst circumstances Billy has a way of being unintentionally comical. August coughs into a fist and I know he's laughing, too.

Sani was the medicine man from the reservation, filling in as the town doctor since Doc James was killed. He'd been filling in for two years and it was beginning to look like he was the permanent replacement. He didn't use the same methods as old Doc, but he was good at what he did. "What news, Billy?" I ask.

"I asked him to look at Sheriff Armstrong's body," he says. "I want to know how he was killed."

This puzzles me. "I assumed he was shot," I say.

Billy shakes his head and I see he's gone pale again. "No, sir," he says. "No bullet wound. His throat was all..." He makes scratching gestures at the sides of his neck. "... Tore up," he finishes. He swallows hard.

"They cut his throat?" I ask. I'm stunned that someone would have gotten the drop on Armstrong like that.

Billy shakes his head. "Not cut," he says. "He bled out through his neck, no question about that, but it weren't no knife that did it. It looked..." Billy glances at

August and I figure Billy has already told him this part. August's face remains passive. Unreadable. Billy wipes his forehead with his sleeve. "It looked torn out, chewed, maybe."

The air in the room seems to drop several degrees. Billy and August both look squirmy. They don't like whatever this is any better than I do. "Billy, are you—" A soft knock on the door interrupts me, and Sani steps in.

His face is solemn as he surveys the room, nodding to August and me. "Deputy Snow," he says in his deep, booming voice, "we must talk." His gaze shifts back to me and August, and I can tell he's not comfortable giving his findings to a civilian and a newspaperman.

"It's all right, Sani," Billy says impatiently. "I've deputized August and John, both. You can tell all of us what you found out."

I'm a little taken aback at the bold lie. Sani holds Billy's gaze until Billy looks away. Somehow, he knows the kid is lying. Still, Sani gives a curt nod and begins to speak.

"Sheriff Armstrong did not go peacefully. His spirit passed due to losing too much blood. He died a warrior, fighting his enemy to the end. There was skin under his fingernails and his knuckles were bruised, indicating the fierce battle he was in."

"Sani, we already knew that." Billy cries in frustration. "What sort of weapon was used?"

Sani again stares at Billy, unblinking. "There was no weapon, not in the way you speak of."

Billy goes a shade whiter. "You mean—"

"Sheriff Armstrong's throat was bitten, Deputy Snow."

Billy takes off his hat and runs a hand through his hair. He is pacing again, mumbling to himself as he does so.

"Sani," I say, "are you positive?"

Sani only nods, looking insulted.

"And they bit deep enough to make him bleed to death?"

Sani nods again. "That is not all," he says gravely.

Billy stops pacing, eyes wide, as though he knows whatever else there is to hear is going to be even worse.

"Sheriff's Armstrong's body was..." Sani pauses, looking up to the ceiling, trying to find the English words. He shakes his head. "There was no blood left in his body."

"You already told us he bled to death," I say. Billy makes a sound I can't identify, and I turn his way. He sort of staggers to one of the chairs against the far wall and sits down hard.

"What is it, Billy?" August asks.

Billy is staring at Sani. "No blood left," he echoes. "None at all, you say?"

Sani shakes his head.

"Billy?" I ask.

He licks his lips and takes a deep breath, letting it out slowly. Shakily. "Other than what blood was used to write that message," he says in a trembling voice, "there wasn't hardly any mess in the house. Just a few drops of blood on the floor."

"Maybe Armstrong was killed outside, and the outlaws dragged his body into the house," August says.

He thinks like a lawman. Again, I wish he'd consider a career change.

Sani is shaking his head emphatically. "They battled in the house," he says. "Some dishes were knocked off the table. A chair was tipped on its side. There were muddy footprints on the floor, indicating a fight."

"What are you getting at, Sani?" I ask. "What happened to all the blood?"

"Chindi," Sani says, then looks skyward and whispers to himself.

I look at Sani, waiting for more. When he doesn't speak, I check the others for any sign of recognition. They are staring at Sani, puzzled looks on their faces. "Sani, what does that mean?" I finally ask.

Sani levels his gaze at me. "Skinwalker," he says.

"Sani," August says coolly, "you can't really—"

Sani turns to him, silencing August with just the force of the expression on his face. "Do not doubt me, Mr. Paulson. White man does not believe in such things, is that right?" Sani steps closer to August, eyes bright with anger. "You do not have to believe," he hisses. "Sheriff Armstrong was killed by a Skinwalker. It drank his blood to steal his strength. It is powerful. And it will kill again."

Billy puts his face in his hands, shaking his head. August is a man who relies on facts. He believes what he sees, what he knows. Billy is the opposite, always keen on the stories at the Last Chance about ghosts or strange creatures wandering the desert. I fall somewhere in the middle. Just because I've never seen a Skinwalker doesn't mean I don't consider it a possibility that they exist. There are all kinds of animals that live in other parts of the world that I know are real even though I've never laid eyes on one. Giraffes and zebras and such. So why not a Skinwalker?

"Sani," I say, "if it is a Skinwalker, what do we do? How do we kill it?"

"John," August says, "you can't—"

I hold up a hand. "We trust Sani to care for everyone here in Sundown. We don't question his medicine even though it's different from Doc's. I think we need to consider what he's telling us."

August opens his mouth to say something but seems to think better of it. He shrugs and gestures for Sani to continue. Billy is back on his feet, wearing a path in the floor.

"It is no easy task," Sani says.

"What do you mean?" I ask. "Surely these Skinwalkers can be killed."

Sani nods. "Yes, they can be killed. But it requires a powerful shaman to perform the ritual."

Billy practically leaps on Sani. "Can you do it?"

Sani shakes his head.

"What about your tribe? Is there a shaman on the reservation that can do the ritual?"

The kid is terrified, and it's a sight I am not accustomed to. I think if someone had written a message to me in blood like the one Billy got, I'd be out of my mind with fear. In that regard, I guess he's doing better than I would be.

Sani seems to consider it. "There is a woman," he finally says.

Billy's expression is a cross between frustration and fear. At first, I think it's because he doesn't want the shaman who might be responsible for saving his life to be a woman.

"Can you get her?" he practically shouts.

I realize it's Sani's slow, deliberate nature that is perturbing him.

"Perhaps," Sani says. Billy looks about ready to explode when Sani goes on. "Powaqa is very wise and once made powerful medicine."

"Wait," Billy says. He points at Sani. "You said 'once made'—what does that mean?"

Sani shrugs, oblivious to Billy's agitation. "Powaqa has seen many seasons. There are those who believe..." Sani taps his forehead. "Some believe she no longer sees the world clearly."

Billy's head snaps between me and August, then his face lights up and he throws his arms in the air. "You mean she's crazy? Loco?"

Sani shrugs again, unimpressed by Billy's animation. "She has moved away from the tribe to be with nature."

"Billy," I say. I need to calm him down. "I think we should listen to what she has to say."

August gives me a cross-eyed look. "John, are you serious? You think some kind of devil murdered Sheriff Armstrong and is now stalking Billy?"

I think about it for a minute. Before the incident with Sheriff Toliver, I probably wouldn't have been so willing to go along with Sani. Now? Well, I know there are things that we don't understand. People who get off on watching things burn and people who need to kill to silence the voices in their head. "I'm willing to keep an open mind about it," I say. "Do you have a better theory on who killed Armstrong and where all his blood ran off to?"

To this, August has no response.

We ride out to Sani's village. It is almost high noon, and the sun is relentless. There is no shade, no relief from its heat. My thoughts keep wandering back to Melanie and Rosie. I don't like leaving them out on the farm by themselves if there is a murderer running around, human or otherwise. Then I remember the way Rosie was at the Last Chance when I was trying to settle a dispute over a card game. I smile. She can take care of herself.

Billy's head never stops moving. It's as if he's trying to look in every direction at the same time.

"Billy," I finally say, "relax, you're going to hurt your neck."

He gives me this blank look, then continues that

constant back-and-forth. Maybe he doesn't realize he's even doing it.

A group of Indians appears out of nowhere, riding bareback and carrying spears and bows. They converse with Sani in their native language for a few minutes. The braves look at us suspiciously, then fall in behind us.

When we reach the village, the looks we get range from curiosity to suspicion to outright hostility. I wonder for the first time if this is a good idea.

"We must go on foot from here," Sani says. He dismounts and lets his horse wander untethered. "You can tie your horse there," he says, pointing to a rudimentary hitching post. "They will be wiped down and watered." He begins walking without waiting for an answer.

We tie off our mounts and follow him as he walks briskly along a barely discernible path, not speaking. The sun beats down incessantly. My throat, already dry from the long horse ride, is parched. I can see August and Billy are in some discomfort as well, but Sani's strides remain powerful, as though he is impervious to the sun and the heat.

I am about to ask how much farther, when we go around a small outcrop of rocks and see a small lean-to built against the north side. Sani gestures for us to wait, then approaches the structure. He calls out in his native tongue and waits. A response comes from within, cracked and dry like the desert floor. He gestures for us to follow, and we do.

The lean-to is built cleverly, surrounding a small, natural cave. It is much larger inside than it appears from the outside. More magic, I think. The interior is also surprisingly cool. It has an aroma I cannot readily identify, some sort of plant or flower, though I see no evidence of either inside.

An ancient, withered husk of a woman sits on the floor cross-legged, watching us with a sharp, knowing gaze as we enter. I'm sure she isn't just looking at me but looking *inside* me. Learning all my secrets, past, present, and future, with that one cunning look. She nods at each of us in turn before speaking to Sani. The light is weak, gloomier than it was when we first walked in.

"Powaqa is willing to help." He pins Billy with his eyes. "She needs you to tell her everything that happened. Do not omit a single thing."

Billy glances nervously at August and me. "Does she understand English?"

"Powaqa understands all language," Sani says.

Billy begins to speak but the woman cries out,

raising a bony arm and gesturing to the area in front of her.

"It is proper to sit with her..." Sani pauses, searching his mind for the right word. "Yadaalti'go," he says, shaking his head in frustration. "...When you converse."

The kid moves tentatively, squatting on the floor in front of Powaqa as if he thinks she might bite. He nods, then takes off his hat. Sani gives him an impatient gesture, urging him to begin.

For the next half hour, Billy tells her everything, beginning to end. A few times, the old woman turns to Sani, and he speaks to her in their language. I assume he's clarifying a word Billy used that she doesn't understand. Mostly, she sits stone-still, her weathered face expressionless. Her eyes, however, are keen. I remember what Sani said about some of the tribe thinking she's too old, and realize how wrong they are.

Finally, Billy says, "That's when Sani here said you might be able to help."

I wait for a response, but she sits motionless. I realize I can barely make her out in the dim light. Has it gotten darker? Powaqa holds her hands out to her sides and begins to whisper. I don't understand her language, of course, but somehow her words are soothing. Any apprehension I felt is gone. The circumstances seem less dire.

I inch my way over to Sani and whisper, "What happens next?"

He doesn't answer. Doesn't even turn his head in my direction. He is fixated on Powaqa, his eyes never moving from her lips. She seems to go on forever. Finally, I realize she has stopped speaking, and when I look, her chin is resting on her chest, her eyes closed.

"Come," Sani says. He moves toward the flap that serves as a door.

"But—" Billy begins but Sani is already gone. He looks to the old woman, starts to say something, then turns and hurries outside. August and I follow.

"Well," Billy says, "is she going to help me?"

Sani's eyes narrow. "Powaqa is a shaman. We go back to town. She will prepare and join us later. Before sunset."

Then he turns and begins that fast-paced walk.

I realize as we trek back to the village that I didn't ask for a drink of water while in Powaqa's lean-to, and we have a long, hot walk back to the horses. I think about all the talking Billy did and wonder what his throat feels like. The sun seems to be at an odd angle. Like we'd been in there a lot longer than it seemed.

When we return to the horses, one of the tribe is waiting there with a deerskin bag filled with ice-cold water. I don't question where it came from or why it is so cold, just drink until I'm quenched. The others do the same. The ride back to town is long and hot. My mind drifts back to Powaqa's lean-to. In my mind's eye, I see her mixing unknown powders and herbs and liquids, sometimes stopping to chant or pray. I wonder what we are getting into.

We reconvene at the sheriff's office, and I realize my stomach is rumbling. I didn't eat lunch and it's probably closer to supper time already. I step outside and wave over one of the Killion boys and tell him to go fetch us some chicken and potatoes from the Last Chance.

While we wait for the food, Billy's distress returns and he begins pacing the floor again. "What is she going to do, Sani?"

"Powaqa is a shaman," Sani repeats.

"I know she is," Billy says, "that's why we went to see her in the first place. I didn't ask what she is, I asked what she is going to do." His tone is calm but mocking, as if he's talking to a child.

Sani doesn't seem to notice, or if he does, he doesn't care. "Powaqa will do what she must."

I dare a look at August and see him trying to hide a smirk. Even though Billy is scared, and the sheriff is dead, Billy's inability to hide his emotions can be humorous, despite the situation.

"Well, isn't that just fine," Billy says, exasperated.

August and I can't help but laugh.

"Relax, Billy," August says. "You're in no worse shape than you were this morning. Besides, we're all here and we'll stay with you until this is over."

The kid looks at August, then turns to me. "Do you mean it? You'll stay?"

I nod. "Of course," I say. It hurts my heart a little. I thought I had left this all behind but that sense of duty I had when I was a deputy didn't get left behind with the badge, I reckon.

The Killion kid—I can never tell those red-headed siblings apart—brings over chicken and potatoes from the Last Chance and the food keeps Billy occupied for a while. I pick at mine, not feeling very hungry. I can't stop thinking about Rosie and Melanie out at the farmhouse. I find myself picturing all sorts of bad things happening, until it about rips me in two.

"I'm going for a walk," I say abruptly, leaving my half-eaten supper on the desk. Billy looks at my plate eagerly. "Go ahead," I tell him, "I'm all finished with it." I've never seen a kid eat so much and stay so thin.

I put on my hat and step out onto the wooden sidewalk, noticing the angle of the sun. Powaqa is supposed to arrive before sunset, but she'll be cutting it close. The sky has already turned an orangey-red, the sun a blinding yellow ball hovering above the mountain tops to the west.

I walk toward the forge, glancing out of habit at the Last Chance for any sign of trouble. It seems quiet. In fact, the whole town seems unusually quiet, as if everyone knows something is going to happen. I push the thought away and step inside the Smitty's shop. Seth Pollon is hammering away at a shoe, sparks flying with each blow. As usual, I stop to marvel at the size of the man, the way the sweat makes his muscles glisten as he swings the heavy hammer.

He senses me watching and looks up. A smile crosses his face, and he gives me a nod. A few minutes later he lifts the shoe with a pair of tongs to examine it, looks satisfied, and plunges it into a bucket of water. The hissing sizzle is accompanied by a cloud of steam. Seth sets the shoe aside, wipes his hands on a rag, and strides over.

"Howdy, John," he says, his deep voice seeming to vibrate through me.

"Howdy, Seth. How is everything?" I do my best not to wince as my hand disappears into his to shake.

"Oh, everything is fine," he says. He smiles again. "Least it was until you walked in. No offense. But I don't think you're here for howdy and to catch up on local gossip."

"No, I guess I'm not," I say.

The big man sighs. "It's about what happened to Sheriff Armstrong, I reckon."

I nod. Seth had proven himself to be brave and trustworthy during the incident with Toliver. He knows I'm calling on him for help again. "Billy came and fetched me this morning," I tell him. "We expect some trouble later and I'll be staying here in town with him and August." I tell him more than I need to, but I trust Seth. At the mention of a Skinwalker, his face pales. He asks a few pointed questions about Armstrong's body, which I'm happy to answer even though I have no idea why he wants to hear the grisly details. "Anyway, August, Sani, and I will be staying at the sheriff's office with Billy tonight. Melanie had a bit of a fever this morning and I'm nervous leaving her and Rosie alone at the ranch."

At the mention of Melanie, Seth's face breaks into a sad smile. It is a reaction I am used to. Melanie had been a pretty little girl before the fire. Somehow, she'd maintained her spirit and kind heart but her looks had not survived so well. Doc, and then Sani, had done their best, but the truth is, Melanie is scarred pretty bad and there's nothing to be done about it.

"You want me to take a ride out and look in on them?" Seth asks.

"I'd sure appreciate that," I say. "But I was wondering if I could impose on you even more. Would you mind accompanying them into town? I'm going to book a room for the night at the hotel. I'll feel better knowing they're nearby and safe. In case they need Sani."

Seth pats me on the shoulder, practically knocking me over. "I'm happy to help, John. I can't stand the thought of that poor girl suffering any more."

"Much obliged, Seth," I say. "Could you head out now? I've got a bad feeling and would be relieved to know they're all settled in before dark."

Seth glances dubiously toward the door. "I reckon I could," he says.

"I'll pay you for any lost wages, for cutting out early, I mean. It's just..." I struggle to find the words, but Seth holds up a big hand to quiet me.

"I understand, John. I'll head out there directly."

I thank him again and head over to the hotel to rent a room. Vance Early is at the desk, writing in an oversized book. The hotel register, I realize a second later. "Howdy, Vance," I say as I approach the desk.

"Why, if it isn't John Pierce," he says with a smile. "Did that good woman finally come to her senses and kick you out?"

I laugh and shake his hand. "I've still got her fooled into thinking I'm the right man for her," I reply. "As a matter of fact, that's why I'm here. I have some business in town, and I'd like a room for Rosie and Melanie while I'm here."

Vance eyes me curiously but I don't say any more. The fewer people that know there's trouble brewing, the better. He flips the page in the register and writes my name. "Just the one night?"

"That should do it." I pay him in advance for the room and tell him Seth will be bringing my wife and daughter shortly. This draws another look, but Vance doesn't press the matter. I nod to him and head back to the sheriff's office.

Billy has finished off every morsel of food and had the Killion kid come back and take the dishes over to the Last Chance. Billy is seated behind the desk, hands on his belly, moaning that he ate too much.

"Where'd you run off to, John?" Billy asks.

"Just taking care of some business," I say. For some

reason I don't want them to know Rosie and Melanie are coming. I'm not sure if it's to try to keep my family safe or so I won't be teased for being so overprotective.

The sound of hoofbeats approaching pulls me from my thoughts. I walk to the door just in time to see Powaqa dismount and tie her horse up. She moves a hell of a lot nimbler than I ever would have expected. She pulls a hefty saddle bag from the back of the horse and throws it over her shoulder. I open the door and hold it for her as Sani rushes out to help her with the bag. She shoos him away with an angry word and he holds his hands up in surrender, following her inside.

Powaqa walks directly to the sheriff's desk, and without hesitation, sweeps aside the piles of papers, spilling some to the floor. Then she begins to carefully lay out a series of objects, holding some of them skyward first and whispering what I assume to be a prayer of some sort.

Many of the items are what I expected: small pouches with who-knows-what inside, crude stick figures, various stones, and a small mortar and pestle. It is the last two items that fill me with dark foreboding. I realize that not only do I not understand what I'm up against, I also have no idea exactly what Powaqa is. These are not the implements of a medicine man—or woman—or of a shaman. At least not from what I've heard during my dealings with Sani's people.

She places the large stone-and-wood mallet on the desk with a thump. Then she holds the deadly-looking wooden stake in two hands and begins to chant in her native language. I glance at the others, but they are all watching Powaqa. I suddenly wish I'd left Rosie and Melanie at the farmhouse.

I pull Sani and the others down the small corridor to where the two cells sit empty. "What the hell is going on?" I demand. "That stake is not medicine or even magic. It's for killing."

Sani holds my gaze calmly, waiting to see if my tantrum is over and done before responding. "Powaqa is sure Sheriff Armstrong was the victim of a Chindi. She has brought the necessary tools to deal with one." He glances at the empty cells and turns back to me with an amused expression. "Did you think you were going to arrest it, Deputy Pierce?"

I pace back and forth in the narrow hall; I must look like Billy. "Are you saying she is going to murder this thing in cold blood?" Sani's face holds his mirth, and a flash of anger makes me wonder how quickly I could wipe that look away.

"Not at all, Deputy Pierce." He turns to Billy. "Deputy Snow will be the one to dispatch the Chindi."

"Me?" Billy exclaims. "Why me?"

"Because you are its intended victim," Sani says. "You have been marked. This gives you more power than the others. A better chance to defeat it."

"But I...I mean, I..." Billy sputters. "I don't know what any of that magic stuff is or how it works."

Sani remains maddeningly calm, as if we were talking about the weather. "Powaqa will instruct you. But when the time comes, it should be you wielding the stake for us to have the best chance to defeat the Chindi." His smirk returns and he adds, "I trust you are able to swing a mallet?"

Billy sighs, looking again to me for help but I have none to offer. "What is this thing going to look like?"

Sani shrugs. "The Chindi, or Skinwalker as you call it, can take on many forms. It may appear as a wild animal, or—" Sani pauses, no longer amused, "—it may look like any one of us."

August has been watching the exchange carefully, studying Sani in particular. He speaks for the first time. "Do you mean it may appear as a human, a man? Because you certainly can't be saying—"

Anger flashes on Sani's face as he steps toward August. "Your disbelief, your doubts, are likely to get us all killed. I am saying what I know to be true of the Chindi. Knowledge passed down by generations of my people, long before you white men came to our land." These words he practically spits out. While August towers over the Sani, he seems to wilt under the man's fury. "The Chindi is as clever as it is brutal and bloodthirsty. It takes every opportunity, every advantage, to carry out its intentions. If it suspects appearing as one of us will be a means to an end, that's what it will do."

Billy and August stare at Sani wordlessly. I've never seen him anything but calm and deliberate. He's treated every sort of injury and illness for the past couple years unflinchingly. This burst of anger, of any emotion, is unprecedented, and none of us know how to react.

Powaqa breaks the tense silence, yelling in her native tongue. I don't understand the words, but her tone is unmistakable. Something is wrong. I move first, rushing back into the office. Powaqa stands motionless, staring out the window. The darkness is complete, the last sliver of daylight has disappeared behind the mountains. She turns, her face grave, and says, "Chalhaheel."

I don't need Sani to translate this time. *Sundown.*

"WHAT IS ALL THIS?" BILLY ASKS, LOOKING AROUND the office. The door and the two windows have something hanging from them. I move closer and confirm. Cloves of garlic. The entire perimeter of the room, save for the threshold of the door, is lined with what looks like salt. There are candles burning, giving off a pungent odor that makes my eyes sting.

Powaqa begins speaking urgently to Sani, gesturing at us, then out the window. Sani nods. "She says the Chindi will come tonight. She has taken the necessary precautions."

"Garlic cloves and salt are the precautions?" August scoffs.

Sani's face hardens. Powaqa glares at August as well, and I realize she understands a lot more English than I understand her language. Or maybe she's just picked up on his tone.

"August," I say sharply. Then I turn to Powaqa. "Why does the salt not protect the door?" Powaqa smiles, sending an icy chill down my spine when I realize the answer.

"Powaqa is not trying to keep the Chindi out," Sani says. "She will seal the door once it is here."

Billy groans. "John, I don't know—"

Powaqa barks out a single word. Sani translates.

"Billy. Get the stake and mallet. Powaqa must ask the Great Spirit for guidance to assist you in your task.

Billy gives me another helpless look, then shuffles to the desk and grabs the weapons. They seem to weigh a thousand pounds the way he carries them to Powaqa. She begins chanting and pulls out a small leather pouch, sprinkling some of the contents over the stake and mallet. Then she dumps the remainder of the powder into the palm of her hand and approaches one of the candles on the desk. She utters more words while looking skyward, then blows the powder into the flame. The room erupts in a blaze of acrid-smelling green smoke.

Powaqa speaks quietly to Sani. "We must extinguish the candles," he translates.

We go around the room doing as instructed. The room is dark, the only light coming from the street torches outside, which isn't much. "Now what?" I ask.

"We wait," Sani says.

He says it as if we're waiting for the stagecoach. His calm is unnerving. Billy starts his pacing, and it goes to work on fraying my nerves. "August, Sani," I say, "why don't you settle in the cells while we wait? We'll take shifts. I'll stay with Billy." I look at Powaqa. "I assume she doesn't sleep?"

Sani gives me a humorless stare. "The Chindi may

come at any time. Things will happen very quickly when it does."

"But it may not come for hours," I say.

Sani shrugs. "Or it may be outside the door right at this moment."

Billy's head snaps toward the door, raising the stake and mallet. August barks out a laugh and I'm thankful for the darkness so Billy can't see my smirk.

"Cocksucker," he mutters.

"Sani," I say, "have you ever faced one of these before?"

"No, but I have seen one. And I have seen its handiwork." I don't want to know the rest, but it's too late to put the cork back in that bottle. "When I was a boy, one came to our village. Children began dying. Withering away like old men and women."

A cold dread seeps into my bones. "Children?"

"The Chindi is ruthless. Smart and clever. Fierce when it needs to be, but sly always. It takes what it needs from the weak, remaining undiscovered for as long as it can."

"What does it take?" August asks.

I answer before Sani does. "Blood."

Sani nods. "It feeds at night, the results often mistaken for disease or famine. Remaining hidden, unknown, is its best protection." He turns to August. "People unwilling to believe it exists are its best allies."

"Then why Sheriff Armstrong?" Billy asks. "Why in that manner, giving itself away?"

I smile to myself. Questions like that are why I know Billy will make a great lawman.

"Vengeance," Sani says. "Your Sheriff Armstrong must have provoked it. Perhaps killed one of its own?"

"Why Billy?" I ask, but again I know the answer.

"The same reason," Sani says, confirming my fear.

I catch August staring at Billy, his expression unreadable. "August?" I say, knowing there's something he isn't telling us.

August sighs and sits on the corner of the desk, hands folded in front of him. "Sani has it right," he says quietly. "I'd been helping Armstrong track down the men that killed Billy's pa and...you know. Armstrong killed one of 'em last week, was going back for the other two." He holds his arms out, palms up. "They must have tracked him down first." He looks sorrowfully at Billy. "He was doing it for you, Billy. He didn't tell you because he didn't want you involved. Thought it would be too hard to face them until there was a set of bars between you and them."

Billy's jaw tightens and a new fire burns in his eyes.

"Now they owe me for another death," he says, in a savage tone I've never heard before.

"Armstrong didn't want to kill 'em," August continues. "He knew you wanted 'em brought in, tried proper. He was trying to do that for you. He respected the hell out of you, Billy. As a lawman. And, well, I think he thought of you as kind of a son."

Billy swallows, and while the fire still burns in his eyes, they're wet with tears. He looks down, takes a deep breath, then lets it out. He straightens, adjusts his gun belt, and says, "Justice will be done. If one or both are... Chindi," his eyes dart to Powaqa, who pays no attention as she holds vigil at the door, "well, it'll be a swifter justice, I reckon."

The moment stretches. I clear my throat. "I still think it would be best if we take shifts. It might be hours yet—" I pause when the room darkens slightly. I look around, taking a minute to figure out that one of the street torches has blown out. I'm about to go on when another goes out and the room darkens by a few more degrees. "I'll check it out," I say, heading to the door with a hand on my revolver. I open the door and step out, swiveling my gaze from side to side. The street is empty, though I can hear some ruckus from the Last Chance. Sure enough, the two torches nearest the office are out. I remain still, waiting. But the air remains dead calm.

I back into the office and close the door. "Two torches out, not a lick of a breeze," I say. "Billy, August, go check the back door." I stay at the window, searching the street for movement. The hairs on the back of my neck shift. Something is about to happen. I suddenly wish I'd asked Seth to stand with us.

"Dead bolt is secure on the back door," Billy calls out. Then, the rest of the street torches go out. Every one, as far as I can see. The darkness is impenetrable. I realize that if we relight the candles or lanterns inside, we are sitting ducks, visible to anyone outside, as if we're on a stage. But if what Sani and Powaqa believe is true, the darkness is its friend. I figure Powaqa would tell us to light them if it was the right thing to do. I step back from the window, unholstering my gun. "Billy, August, get ready."

I hear the smooth sound of Billy's shooter coming out of its holster. Then the mechanical sound of August cracking the shotgun I'd given him, checking it for shells for the hundredth time, then slamming it shut. "Keep that thing pointed at the back door, August. Billy and I have the front. Sani? You sure you won't take a gun?"

"No gun," Sani says, but for the first time he sounds doubtful.

There is nothing but darkness beyond the windows and again I consider snuffing the candles. Then the windows explode in a shower of broken glass, and hell comes to Sundown.

THE ROOM ERUPTS IN A CHAOS OF GUNSHOTS AND screaming. A shape - I think it is a wolf or coyote, though it makes no sense - barrels into my chest. I'm knocked backward, flipping over the desk as I empty my revolver. In that split-second of contact, I see Rosie and Melanie huddled together in the hotel room. Then I blink and I'm struggling to my feet. The ruckus seems to last forever but it's over in less than a minute. Sani lights a lantern and as the gun smoke clears, I try to assess the damage. August is dead, or will be in short order, his throat ripped open and spraying blood into a widening pool on the floor. Billy's hurt bad, his arm hanging by skin and muscle, almost torn off. Sani, who looks unharmed, is tending to him. Powaqa also seems untouched by the violence.

At first, I think I've made it unscathed, then I see the blood dripping at my feet from a triple row of gashes in my stomach. Claw wounds, I realize. I rip my shirt open and take stock. Deep and ugly, but not fatal.

The other casualty lies in a heap by the door. I don't recognize him, and I doubt anyone else will. Most of his face is gone, courtesy of a shotgun blast from August. It looks like the other barrel got him in the leg, which is no longer attached to the rest of him. August gives a final gurgle, twitches once, then is still.

"Is he gonna make it?" I ask Sani.

He doesn't respond but continues working on staunching the copious amount of blood leaving Billy's shoulder. Powaqa joins him and they speak in urgent voices but in their native tongue.

I move to the door and look up and down the street. There were two of them that came through the window. The second one fled during the gunfire. I see a trail of blood leading down the street. I turn to tell Sani I'm going after him when movement catches my eye.

The one I thought was dead, miraculously, is not. He's trying to get to his feet - or foot - and his one eye is darting wildly about the room. It finds Billy and he starts to crawl toward him. It's impossible, but it's happening. Then I remember the mallet and stake. I see both objects on the floor and lunge for them. I scoop them off the floor and spin to face the crawling man—

In his place, a three-legged wolf is crouched, ready

to spring at Billy. I leap just as it does, and meet it in mid-air, landing heavily on top of it. It thrashes wildly, growling and snapping its teeth. I manage to get a forearm across its throat and pin it down.

Sani leaves Billy's side and holds it down while I adjust my grip on the stake and place it against the beast's chest. Sani nods and I bring the hammer down with all my might, ignoring the pain as the cuts on my stomach rip open wider.

The blow drives the stake deep into the creature's body, and blood sprays from the wound and from the wolf's nose and mouth. Then it is still. Sani rushes back to work on Billy and I roll off to the side, grasping my wounds and cringing at the slick, hot blood that is flowing out of me. I tear off the rest of my shirt and press it to the wound.

"We can't save the arm," a voice says, and I realize I must have passed out. It's Sani, still tending to Billy. The room goes all shimmery for a minute, then Billy's scream snaps me back to full consciousness. I struggle to my feet, still pressing the soggy shirt into my gut, and turn away in horror. Billy's arm is now tossed to the side of the room while Sani and Powaqa work to cauterize the gaping wound that was his shoulder.

I take a gasping breath, trying to make sense of what I'm looking at. Where I'd driven the stake into the wolf's chest lies the man with half a face. It's all true, I think. He was a Skinwalker. The stake protrudes from his chest as the final proof. I stagger over to the desk and find my revolver, reloading with shaky hands. I take the shotgun that August had used and reload that as well. "Sani, I'm going after him. I'll send Seth over to help you." I look around the office. August dead in a puddle of congealing blood. The other one with a stake sticking out of his chest. And Billy, poor Billy. "Clean up," I say.

"Deputy Pierce," Sani calls. I pause. "Your bullets will not kill the Chindi. As you have seen."

I sigh. "It's all I have," I say.

Powaqa speaks and Sani listens, then says, "Silver. Powaqa says she has heard tales that silver kills the beasts, though she has not seen it for herself."

I nod and leave the office. I look again up and down the street, then start following the trail of blood. It's easy at first but then it dissipates to drops spread farther and farther apart. "The bleeding is stopping," I mutter, picturing the way the other one got up even with half its head gone. After another twenty feet, the trail stops. I'm close to the blacksmith's, where Seth lives above the shop. I pound on his door, rousing him from sleep, but he's more than eager to help. I offer him the shotgun but he's already holding his Winchester. I guess he figured good news doesn't come knocking in the middle of the night.

I give Seth a very brief description of what happened and tell him I'm going after the other one. He gawks at my wound but says nothing, then heads to the sheriff's office. I search the dusty road for a continuation of the blood trail. It's gone, as if the bleeding just stopped. I look in the direction he—*it?* —was heading, and freeze. The strange image of Melanie and Rosie in the hotel room flashes in my head. "Shit!" I break into a run toward the hotel.

I burst through the door and dart toward the front desk. Vance Early is staring at me, one hand under the desk, probably clutching a shotgun. "John, what is it now?"

His question takes me by surprise, and I stop. "What do you mean?"

His expression is one of sheer confusion. "Y-you came in a few minutes ago..."

Terror rips through me as Sani's words echo in my head. *The Chindi, or Skinwalker as you call it, can take on many forms. It may appear as a wild animal, or, it may look like any one of us.* "What room, Vance?" I ask, heading for the stairs.

"I already told you, number nine," he yells. "What is going on?"

I'm already up the steps and running down the hall. The door to nine is open. Just as I approach, I hear a scream, followed by a gunshot. I'm too late.

The scene before me is impossible. Melanie is crouched on the bed behind Rosie. She is holding her derringer, pointed at the body on the floor. For a split-second, I am looking at my own dead body, a bullet hole right between my eyes. Then I blink and it's not me, but a dead body all the same. A stranger.

I step toward Rosie, but she swings the derringer in my direction. I can see the muscles in her forearm twitching. I don't know how many pounds of pressure her little gun takes, but she's within a hair of it. "Don't take another step," she says, her voice shaky but firm.

"Daddy!" Melanie says, but I realize it's a question.

"Rosie," I say, keeping my hands raised by my sides. I look down at the body again, but it's still a stranger. I understand what happened, that the Skinwalker had appeared as me. It explains Vance's confusion and why my wife is pointing a gun at me, and why my daughter isn't sure I'm actually me. "I came directly from the sheriff's office after we killed the other one." I shift my eyes again to the body. "The other Chindi. Skinwalker." I recall the way the one in the office looked dead then went after Billy. My hand instinctively goes for my gun, but Rosie stops me.

Her shout would stop anyone. "Don't!"

"Rosie," I say, "you don't understand. Bullets don't kill them. It's not dead." My eyes dart wildly back and forth between her and the body on the floor. I know it will come to, and change. Go after her again. I take a deep breath but keep my eyes on the body. "I had to put a stake through the other one's heart. August shot it in the head, and we thought it was dead, but—" I risk a look at her and am shocked to see a knowing grin on her face. "What?" I ask.

"What's my mother's name?" Rosie asks.

I stare at her, knowing what she's doing. Damn, she's a smart woman. I open my mouth to answer but realize with horror that I can't remember the name.

Rosie and I had spent a lot of long, quiet nights at the farmhouse, sharing stories about our past. We met each other late in life and had a lot of catching up to do. A lot of getting to know one another. I remember every story she'd told me about her mother—who wasn't the nicest person in the world based on those stories - but the name won't come. "Rosie, I...I can't remember."

To my surprise, she smiles and lowers the pistol. "That's 'cause I never told you," she says, and leaps into my arms. Melanie joins her, jumping off the bed and wrapping herself around my legs. As happy as I am, I can't hug them back. I struggle from their grasp and pull my gun, keeping it trained on the guy's head.

"John," Rosie says, putting a gentle hand on my arm and pushing it down. "It's dead." Before I can respond, she pops the second bullet out of the derringer. I gape at the object in her hand. It's silver. "Seth brought them over, he spent most of the evening making them in his shop."

"But...how did he know?" Even Sani and Powaqa weren't sure silver would work.

Rosie grinned. "Seth knows all about Skinwalkers," she says. "They don't call them that, or...whatever you called them."

"Chindi," I say absently.

"But whatever Seth's people call them, it sounds like the same thing."

"The devil," Melanie whispers, and I can't find it in me to disagree.

We all go back to the sheriff's office after telling Vance not to go into room nine. I realize I'm still shirtless and wonder what a scene I must have made, showing up at the hotel like that. My wounds are still bleeding freely, and Sani pulls me into the back and lays me on one of the cots.

Powaqa joins him, handing me a mug of some rancid-smelling liquid. She gestures for me to drink, and I do it without question. After what I've seen tonight, I will never doubt her or Sani again.

Sani takes my gun belt and hands it to me. "Bite down on this when the pain is too great. What Powaqa gave you will help, but you will still feel this."

I hear Sani's words but look at the belt, not comprehending. The room goes a little swimmy and he lays me back on the cot. I close my eyes and though I feel a little pain and some tugging on my wounds, I don't need the belt.

I open my eyes, realizing I must have dozed off. I stare in amazement at the zigzags that run across my wounds. Sani enters, offering a rare smile when he sees me awake. "What did you do?" I ask.

Sani looks puzzled. "We stopped the bleeding. Acacia awns to hold the wound together until it heals."

I gape at the crisscross pattern on my gut. "I'll be," I

say. "Doc would have packed the wounds with gunpowder."

Sani shakes his head in disgust.

"Billy?" I ask.

Sani's face hardens. "He lost a lot of blood before we were able to stitch the wounds." He gestures towards my stomach. "It is out of our hands."

I start to sit up but Sani rushes to my side and pins me with his hands. "Not yet, Deputy Pierce. Too much movement will break the stitches."

"Help me up, Sani," I say.

Sani holds my gaze for a second, as though he's going to argue, then seems to understand I'm getting up with or without his help. He reaches over and swings my legs toward the floor. "Try not to bend," he says, then pulls me to my feet.

He is not a big man, so his strength is surprising. It seems to take little effort for him to pull me upright. I wince and reach for the stitches, but he pushes my hand away.

"Do not touch."

"Thank you, Sani. For me and Billy." I put a hand on his shoulder.

Sani nods. "I must check on Deputy Snow."

I follow him to the next cell. Billy is motionless on the cot. He is not conscious, but I see the rise and fall of his chest. I've never seen a man as pale as this. It's hard to tell where his face ends and the white pillow begins. There is a sheet pulled up to his chin and a noticeable flatness where the bump of his arm should be. I swallow hard. Even if he pulls through, it's going to be hard days ahead for him.

I go out to the main office and approach Seth. The big man is gaping at the scene around him. The broken window, August's body, the other dead body with the stake sticking out of it, Billy's arm...it's a living nightmare. But it could have been so much worse.

"I don't know how to thank you," I say, my eyes stinging. "If you hadn't made those bullets—" He cuts me off by wrapping me up in a hug. It doesn't feel very manly, but it's just what I need.

"You and Rosie are my friends," he says, pulling away. "And little Melanie." He smiles at her, and she gives him her own heartbreaking smile right back. "I'd do just about anything for that little angel."

Powaqa breaks the moment by speaking to Sani in her language, then starts to pack up all the stuff she'd brought. "Powaqa will return home now," Sani translates.

"Now?" I exclaim. "In the dark?"

Sani offers a ghost of a smile. "She has the stars to guide her," he says.

"Still," I say, "we could put her up at the hotel—"

Sani laughs. "She would never sleep in a building such as that," he says.

She is packed up and heading for the door. I call her name and she turns. "Thank you, Powaqa. You saved a lot of good people tonight. I appreciate it. If you ever need anything—" She nods, and then she is gone. A moment later, I hear hoofbeats fading away.

"I guess I'd better set to getting this mess cleaned up," I say.

"How's he doing, Sani?" It's been two weeks since we faced the Skinwalkers, and Sani is taking out the acacia awns he used to sew up the gashes on my stomach. I'm in Doc James's old place, where Sani has taken what appears to be permanent residence as town doctor.

"Deputy Snow is young and strong," Sani replies. "He will survive."

"That's good," I say, wincing as Sani works on me. "But how is he dealing with..." I can't bring myself to say it.

Sani gives me a look, but he knows what I mean. "He is adapting quickly. He is—"

The door opens and Billy steps in. It's jarring to see him with only one arm. He looks pale and a little thin, but his smile is real. "Howdy, John. Melanie and Rosie said you were here."

"How are you, Billy?" I ask.

He looks toward the empty space where his arm used to be. "I reckon my juggling career is over and I can only swim in circles, but I'm getting along."

I laugh, knowing I could never be that casual about losing an arm. But I know Sani is right: Billy is strong, and he'll adapt.

"Town council is voting this week," Billy says, his demeanor changing.

After losing two sheriffs in as many years, the council is voting on appointing Billy as acting sheriff until the next election. That's the other reason I'm back in Sundown today. I plan to get the ear of the council members and make sure they do right by him. "I guess that means I'll be calling you Sheriff Snow pretty soon."

Billy blushes and shuffles his feet.

"John, your wounds are healing and there is no sign of infection." Sani steps back, throwing the awns in the trash next to the bed. "They will itch, but you must not scratch, or they will open again."

"Thank you, Sani," I say, getting to my feet. "Is there anything I can do for you? Or Powaqa?"

Sani shakes his head. "We are both doing well, John. But there may come a day when one of us does need your assistance." He offers a thin smile.

I nod, not sure what he means or what help I could give either one of them, but I know better than to ask. Sani is a man of few words and he'll tell me what he needs when he needs it. "What do you gentlemen say to lunch?"

Billy's face lights up. Other than being a lawman, food is just about Billy's favorite thing. Sani apologizes but says he has other patients to call on. Billy and I walk over to the blacksmith's shop to say hi to Seth. The big man is hard at work on the forge, as always. After exchanging pleasantries, we head over to the Last Chance.

I order a beer but Billy refuses to drink alcohol while he's on duty. Rosie and Melanie join us as planned and we order steaks. We laugh a lot during the meal, and once again I'm amazed at the amount of food Billy can put away. He entertains Melanie with some magic tricks, and it warms my heart to see her smile and laugh so much.

While I love Billy's company, I don't miss wearing the badge. My life on the farm with Rosie and Melanie is everything I've ever wanted. After the meal, I call on the members of the council to voice my support for Billy.

Finally, the three of us climb up on the wagon and I shake the reins to get the horses going. The sun is sinking toward the mountains in the west, the way it always has and always will. But there's something different about it after what we went through. It's not as pretty as it used to be. I reckon I'll always wonder what else is out there in the world. After the Skinwalkers, I guess just about anything is possible. I turn to Rosie and Melanie and smile. For now, the two of them and the farm are the only things I need.

ACKNOWLEDEMENTS

First and foremost, thank you to the team at Cemetery Dance for taking a chance on my Old West horror stories. I had a lot of fun writing them and I hope everyone enjoys reading them.

A big THANK YOU and my undying appreciation for the red pen of Linda Nagle. Her edits made these stories what they are.

As always, I owe most of the credit to my wife and best friend, Sheila. Her endless patience with my visits to Tombstone and putting up with all our stops at ghost towns and abandoned mines across the country are a big reason these stories exist.

Of course, thank you to my readers, old and new. These stories are for you.

Tom Deady
November, 2024